WHIRLWIND

Hohanonivah — a Cheyenne orphan whose name means 'whirlwind' — is taken in as a child by Patrick and Esther Jackson, who raise him as their son. When, years later, his adoptive parents are murdered, Hohanonivah swears a solemn oath that those who took the elderly couple's lives will die by his hand. Tracking down the men responsible, he finds himself facing two of the most ruthless outlaws in the state — Jed and Eli Holt, psychopathic brothers who will kill for the most trifling of reasons . . .

FENTON SADLER

WHIRLWIND

Complete and Unabridged

LINFORD
Leicester

First published in Great Britain in 2014 by
Robert Hale Limited
London

First Linford Edition
published 2016
by arrangement with
Robert Hale Limited
London

A catalogue record for this book is available
from the British Library.

ISBN 978–1–4448–2827–6

Published by
F. A. Thorpe (Publishing)
Anstey, Leicestershire

Set by Words & Graphics Ltd.
Anstey, Leicestershire
Printed and bound in Great Britain by
T. J. International Ltd., Padstow, Cornwall

This book is printed on acid-free paper

Prologue

Colorado, 29 November 1864

The cavalry rode into the encampment, disregarding both the white flags of surrender waved by the Cheyenne and also the single great American flag which had been raised at the centre of their village and around which dozens of Indians huddled for protection, believing that the white soldiers would respect this emblem of their own nation. They were mistaken. The bluecoats opened fire with carbines and then followed up by hacking at the survivors with their sabres. They were apparently determined to leave no survivors: men, women or children. Twenty or thirty women and their children had taken refuge in a little gully, but the troopers set about killing them as well.

Lieutenant Carson dismounted and wandered through the Cheyenne village in a daze, unable to make sense of the scene before him. Men whom he knew well were trying to ravish young Indian women, while others were firing indiscriminately into a group of mothers with their children clinging to them. A small boy, lighter-skinned than the other children and no more than seven or eight years of age, stood bewildered and alone outside one of the tepees. Without thinking, Carson grabbed his arm and began dragging him in the direction of the supply wagons. He tried to make it look as though he were behaving as brutally as the other soldiers. The child did not resist.

When they reached the nearest wagon, Carson lifted the boy up and placed him inside, concealed from the outside world by the large canvas hood. He said to the boy, 'Do you speak English? Can you understand me?' There was no reply. The lieutenant pushed the boy down until he was lying flat and then pulled some rugs over him. 'Stay here, you understand? Don't move!' Although the child had said nothing, nor even indicated whether or not he knew what Carson was saying to him, he stayed low and made no effort to sit up.

Lieutenant Carson of the 3rd Colorado Cavalry went back to the village and attempted to instil some discipline into the men and restore order. It was a hopeless enterprise. They were in a frenzy of debauchery and none of the other officers showed any inclination to call a halt to the outrages. When darkness came, Carson went back to the wagon and was mildly surprised to find the Indian boy still lying there quietly. He handed the boy half a loaf of bread and a canteen of water and then harnessed up the wagon, heading for the nearest farmhouse that he could find. He had no idea what fate would befall any other survivors of the massacre that day, but he was determined that one child at least would be saved.

Ten or eleven miles down the track, in the opposite direction from Denver City, Carson came across a farmhouse. It was a soddie built of cut turfs, with a large wooden extension to one side. He pulled up and hailed the occupants. Lamplight showed through one of the windows and so he suspected that those inside were not yet sleeping. He was right, because after a space, a man who looked to be about sixty came out of the house, holding aloft a barn lantern.

'Who are you and what are you wanting?' cried the man.

'I have a child here. I want somebody to care for him.'

'A child? This makes strange listening. Are you sure you are not about some villainy? If so, you'd best take care, my partner has you covered from the window.'

'Nothing of the sort. It is an Indian boy. I cannot keep him with me.'

4

'Come down then. Mind, you'd best keep your hands where we can see them.'

Lieutenant Carson climbed down and then went to the back of the wagon. The boy was sitting up and looking round him warily. 'Come on son, there's nothing to be afeared of.' He reached up and the boy suffered himself to be lifted down from the wagon and set on the ground.

The man with the lamp had come closer and was staring in perplexity at Carson and the Indian boy. 'Soldier, is it? And an Indian? What's the game?'

'No game, sir. This boy's family are dead and I need somebody to care for him. Will you do it?'

The man stared at the child intently. At length he said, 'Bring him into the house.'

The man's 'partner' was indeed in the house and covering the scene outside. She was a grey-haired woman of about the same age as he, that is to say sixty or more. She was holding a

5

shotgun, but set it against the wall as soon as she caught sight of the child. She and the man were looking in wonder at the little boy. Carson repeated his hope of finding shelter for the boy. She said, 'Are you saying that you want us to care for this child? For how long?'

The lieutenant cleared his throat. 'Well forever, I guess or leastways until you can find somebody else to take on the job. I have to get back. Will you take this child in charge and care for him?'

'As God knows, we will,' said the woman. 'The Lord has guided you here with this charge.'

'I know aught of that, ma'am,' said the soldier, suddenly embarrassed at hearing the Deity mentioned in this matter-of-fact way, 'but if you will look after the fellow, then that is enough for me.'

The old man took Carson's hand and squeezed it hard. 'You may rest easy. We shall protect this child and raise him as though he were our own. God bless you, son, for this.'

The lieutenant jumped up on to his wagon and turned it round, heading back to Sand Creek, hoping that he had done the right thing.

1

Han Jackson sat on an outcrop of rock about a half mile from the soddie, watching his parents as they moved about the vegetable garden back of the house. They were slower than they had been even a year ago and looked increasingly frail and helpless to the young man. He hated to leave them alone, even for a day, but they had both insisted that he go off into the wilderness for a spell, as tradition required.

Devout Methodists as they were, his adoptive parents had always done their best to ensure that the child to whose care they had pledged themselves did not lose touch with his own origins. They were hardened in this resolve by what they later discovered of the massacre which had left the child an orphan. He had learned English, but never been allowed to forget his own language or the ways of his forefathers. They took him on regular trips to Cheyenne villages, where he learned about the tribe from which he had come.

Today Han, as everybody knew him, was to go into the wilderness for a week with no food or water and survive only on what he could find for himself. He was eighteen or thereabouts and it was important that he undertake this test of stamina before he was much older.

Patrick and his wife had stopped hoeing and were taking a rest by the side of the little garden which was Esther's pride and joy.

'That boy's still fretting about leaving us by ourselves for a few days,' observed Esther, in a tone which she tried to make impatient but which her husband knew very well expressed pride and affection. 'He acts like we can't get along without him for more than a day. Young fool.'

'He worries about us,' her husband

said. 'As God he knows, we are neither of us as spry as once we were. You have to admit that, Esther.'

His wife laughed shortly. 'Then what? We are both over seventy. I can still keep house and you can still plough a field. Ain't that enough?'

'He's coming down from yonder rock. Mark what I say, he'll be telling us that he sees no need for this final stage and that since he aims to run this farm, it does not signify that he can pass all the tests that a young Indian brave might need to undertake.'

Hohanonivah Jackson or Han as he was invariably known, at least among white folk, was a striking figure. Working on the farm alongside his adoptive father had given him an astonishingly muscular physique for his age and he was as tall and graceful as any Indian warrior. His hair, which he had lately allowed to grow right down over his collar, was that lustrous and glossy black which appears to have a touch of blue in it when the light catches it at a certain angle. High cheekbones and a clear, copper-coloured skin completed the picture.

When once he reached his parents, Han squatted down between them, putting his arms around their shoulders and kissing each lightly on the top of the head. Esther pretended to be irritated by this display of affection.

'What are you about, child? Have you gone soft?' she demanded gruffly. The young man grinned back at her, love showing in his eyes.

'I am going to miss the two of you over the next week. I wanted to tell you so.'

'Well, well, that's enough now,' said the old woman, briskly. 'You are ready to start out this afternoon?'

'Are you sure that . . . ' Han's words tailed off. He was gripped by an uneasiness; a nameless fear that something would befall these two good people if he were not there to care for them. He never talked of the massacre at Sand Creek, but the memory of it still lingered within him. If only he had been able to save his real mother from the barbarians who had cut her down in front of his eyes.

'Off you go now son,' said Patrick Jackson. 'We'll manage well enough without you for a while.' The boy gazed for a moment or two into the old man's eyes and then nodded and went off to the house to prepare.

When you are only eighteen, anything that happens to you is likely to seem like an adventure and Han Jackson's week in the wild was no exception. He had slept outside before, so that was no great hardship; as for catching his own food and finding water, these too proved easy enough. He was able to start a fire by using the traditional methods and tracking down lizards and snakes was something he had been doing since he was small. His unerring aim at throwing even enabled him to bring down a couple of jackrabbits with rocks, which he skinned and roasted alongside the lizards.

Han, short for Hohanonivah or *Whirlwind* in Cheyenne, was guiltily aware that this expedition was supposed to be somewhat more than a camping trip. It was a time of reflection; he should be trying to commune with the Great Spirit during this retreat, but he had received no messages from the gods and so took it that he was just not one of those so favoured. He remembered though to make his prayers each night to the God of his parents, thanking him for His mercy. Due to his raising, he saw no contradiction at all in praying to Jesus one night and then the next day invoking the gods of his ancestors.

All in all, the week passed pleasantly and uneventfully enough, although Han felt a little leaner and more tired by the end of the time. He was surely looking forward to sleeping in a proper bed again. At dawn on the final day, he set off back towards the valley, reaching the hills which rose above it a little before noon. He climbed over the ridge and saw his home laid out below him, the

13

neat patchwork of fields surrounding the house. As he looked more closely at the scene beneath him, something struck him as strange. Near the house he could see what at first he took to be bundles of clothes. Not only that, although it was mid-morning, he could see no sign of either of his parents. Then, in a flash, it became clear. What he had taken to be clothes were really two figures lying on the ground.

Han started to run down the side of the rocky hillside towards his home. In his mind he went frantically over the things which could have happened to the elderly couple. Perhaps they had fallen ill and collapsed? If so, then he might be in time to get them into bed and care for them. He cursed himself for leaving them alone. He knew now that those bad feelings he had had about this scheme of going off for a week had been a warning to him. If only he had heeded it!

As he got closer, he checked his headlong rush and stopped to look a little harder at the figures of his parents. They would hardly both have fallen ill and collapsed at the same moment right close to each other like that. He drew the razor-sharp knife from its sheath and set off at a slower trot, his eyes constantly scanning the surroundings for anything at all out of the ordinary. By the time he got down to the valley, he knew already that they were dead.

As he approached the man and woman lying in the dirt, he could see clouds of flies buzzing around them. There could be no doubt that they had died some while ago. When he got up close, the full horror of the thing hit him. The man he called his father had been shot several times in the back and his wife had, from the look of her, had her throat cut. Hohanonivah stood there for a good few minutes trying to figure out what had happened in his absence.

If he had been a sheriff or marshal, then he would perhaps have wondered if one had not killed the other and then committed suicide. Knowing them as he did though, Han knew instinctively that this was no sort of explanation. He walked round the bodies slowly, looking for signs of what might have happened. Whatever it was, it must have happened right here: there was no sign of the bodies being dragged about; they had almost certainly died right where they lay. Died! At the thought of this, the young man could restrain himself no longer and he fell to his knees, weeping hopelessly like a bereft child.

The death of these people, who had been so precious to him, inevitably put Hohanonivah in mind of the massacre in his childhood, during the course of which he had lost his first parents. He remembered the feeling of sheer helplessness as he watched his mother being killed. What he would have given, young as he was, to be able to strike at the bluecoat who had cut her down. But at that time he had been a child, maybe eight years old. He could have done nothing against those savages. It was different now.

Eventually, Han got to his feet and went into the house. He saw at once that the floorboards had been pulled up and the clay jar where his parents hid their money had been removed. It lay smashed on the floor and of the gold coins which it had contained, there was no sign. A glint beneath the floorboards caught his eye. Two of the $10 pieces had fallen there and been missed by the thieves. He reached down and picked them up. Nothing else seemed to be missing. He went back outside.

There had been no rain for the last week or more and so the tracks of the horses which had ridden up to the house were still fairly clear. It looked to Han as though there had been four or five of them. He couldn't imagine five men coming here especially for his parents' meagre savings; they must just have been passing and decided on the off-chance to see if there was anything here worth stealing. Obviously both

Patrick and Esther Jackson would have taken that ill and so they had been killed. He went back to the house and returned with a spade.

It took the young man most of the afternoon to dig the two graves deep enough. When he had done so, he lifted the bodies of the old people reverently and laid them carefully in their last resting place. Then he fetched the Bible from the house. Han read a few passages from the New Testament; those relating to the promise of eternal life. Then he closed the Bible and said out loud,

'Hear my words, all gods and spirits. I will hunt down those who murdered these good people and kill them with my own hands. I shall not rest for anything until everyone who had a hand in this is dead.'

While Hohanonivah Jackson was burying his parents, the men who had killed them were some sixty miles away, heading south towards New Mexico at a leisurely pace. Threatening an old couple into revealing the hiding place of their wealth and then killing them anyway was not something likely to weigh heavily on the consciences of four of the five riders. Only one of the men looked troubled and anxious, as though what passed for a conscience in him was raising its head. Every one of the men, this one included, had plenty of bad deeds to their credit. Still, although the murders had only been committed two days ago, only he was still thinking of them. The band he was riding with had been in need of some cash money and did not feel much inclined to leave any witnesses behind who might later be able to identify them. Only one of them though was still gnawing away at what had been done. His unease had not gone unnoticed by two of the other riders.

Eli Holt and his brother Jed were in a sense the leaders of the group who were making their way to New Mexico. The two brothers had picked up with the other three members of the band while engaged in some road agent work up in Wyoming. The other men had been overawed by what they had seen of the Holts in action and felt that here were men who would stop at nothing in the pursuit of easy money and lively action. Eli and Jed were both as keen on gunplay and fist fighting as they were on any actual spoils and anybody tagging along with them could be sure that they would have little time to grow restless or bored. Where the brothers were, excitement and bloodshed were never far behind.

The five men had worked their way south from Wyoming, leaving in their wake a trail of robberies, rapes, assaults and murder. Their aim now was to move into New Mexico and prey on the Comancheros who worked out of that territory. This was apt to be a dangerous undertaking, but if they were successful, the plunder would be considerable. Their three followers were not aware of the fact, but there was a pretty high turnover in membership of the Holt Gang. This was because the brothers generally found a way of sacrificing their men in order to save their own skins when the going got tough. Those who rode with the Holts had an alarming tendency to get shot or taken by the law before the time came to share out the spoils. Had they been a little brighter, the three men now riding with Eli and Jed might have asked themselves how come such a bloody and resourceful pair of characters had been riding alone when they teamed up with them. You would have thought that such men would have gathered around them a regular gang long since.

* * *

Han's pony was hungry but otherwise healthy. She had been in the field with a plentiful supply of water but little in the way of food other than the scrubby, dry grass. He saddled her up and then packed a bag with some food. He had a rifle of his own and also tucked his father's pistol into his belt. Last of all, he brought out the quiver and bow which he had made with his own hands as custom dictated. The bow he carried slung across his back and the quiver of arrows he attached to the saddle.

Then he went back into his home a final time and opened the Bible again at the Book of Hosea. When he had been little, his parents told him that he was mentioned in the Good Book, and they pointed out the verse in Hosea which makes reference to the whirlwind. Now he spoke this same verse out loud, as a promise and perhaps prophecy. In a strong, clear voice, he said, 'They that sow the wind shall reap the whirlwind.' He closed the Bible and set it gently on the kitchen table. In a quieter voice, he said, 'Those bastards have surely sown the wind. Let's see if they are ready to reap the whirlwind.' Following which reflection, he locked the door behind him, mounted the pony and set off south in pursuit of his prey.

2

Once Han was clear of the farm and on the open trail, he could read the tracks of the men he was pursing a little clearer. Back at the farm they had been mixed up and overlying each other, but now he could plainly distinguish one from the other: five riders, of that there was no doubt. He dismounted and peered closely at the hoof marks. There were Cheyenne who had been raised to this game who might be able to deduce everything from those marks in the dirt up to and including the colour of the riders' hair and what they had had for breakfast, but Han was not all that much of a tracker. He could just about discern that the horses had been in no hurry and proceeding at a pretty leisurely trot, but that was all. That and the fact that these were big horses, shod by white men. This did not prove of course that the riders were white, but it was a clue.

Han rode on, sometimes at a trot but mostly at a canter, for two hours. Dusk was setting in and he was wondering where he might camp for the night. Off to his left, he saw the flicker of a small fire. It was unlikely to be the men he was pursuing as they would surely be much further ahead by now, but even so he decided to take a look. It was just possible that they had finished some business in the south and were heading back again. He dismounted and led the pony alongside some rocks, hoping to approach the fire quietly.

About a mile from the camp-fire, Han realized that there was no need for caution. A man had begun chanting; an eerie sound that carried clearly to Han on the still, evening air. These were Cheyenne! He remounted and trotted forward towards the camp.

There were seven young men seated around the fire and one standing up; presumably the one who had been

24

declaiming a spirit chant. They watched as Han approached. He must have made a strange sight. Although obviously Indian, he was dressed in white men's clothes, the only concession to his own origins being the bow, quiver of arrows and his long hair, which was held back by a beaded headband.

Han pulled up a few yards from the men who were all in their early- or mid-twenties. Judging by the amount of weaponry lying around, these were dog soldiers who belonged to a military caste and followed a code of chivalry as strict as that of the Japanese samurai. There had been a number of skirmishes with the army lately and these men were some of the fighting force of the Cheyenne. He wondered what they would make of an Indian dressed in white man's clothes, but he needn't have worried. The men had apparently heard of him. The one who was standing up greeted him.

'You are . . . Whirlwind?'

He had hesitated for a moment,

because among themselves, some of the dog soldiers had another name for Hohanonivah. They called him 'The boy who learned to be white'. This was not the sort of name to use to a man's face however, leastways not unless you wanted to provoke a deadly quarrel.

Han climbed off his mount and made the signs of greetings to the men, saying, 'I am Whirlwind. The Great Spirit has smiled on the hour of our meeting, my brothers.' He wondered if he had overreached himself. He was not technically a warrior and perhaps using the word 'brothers' had looked like boasting to them. If so, then they didn't give any sign. Instead, the man who was standing invited Han to sit down and share meat with them.

His command of Cheyenne was good enough for him to be able to follow most of the conversation between the seven men. Han gathered that they had been in a skirmish with the bluecoats and were now heading north towards a meeting with other bands of warriors under the leadership of Dull Knife. At length, they asked him what he was doing and where he was going. He told them of the death of his parents, which caused shaking of heads and expressions of regret. The Jacksons had lived in Cheyenne territory for forty odd years and had always been neighbourly with any man, red or white. Esther had helped deliver babies and Patrick had run lessons at some villages. Although they were Christians, they never tried to draw anybody to their religion, believing as they did that there was only one God and whether he was worshipped as the Great Spirit of the Indians or the Lord of Hosts of the Bible it made little difference.

'Do you know who did this?' asked one of the men.

'No. There were five men and they are going south. I thought you might have seen them.'

'White men? Five?'

'I don't know if they are white. I think so.'

'We have seen them, but they have not seen us. I know two of them. They have been here before. You need to be careful. These are wolves.'

The Cheyenne word that the young man used was *ho'nehe*, which means literally *wolf*. However, in idiomatic use it conveyed a man who had the soul of a beast. It was not a flattering term, but told Hohanonivah all that he needed to know.

'How long since you passed them?'

'Two days. You will need to ride hard to overtake them.'

'I will ride hard. And I will overtake them and then kill them all.'

This was the sort of talk which was pleasing to the ears of the young men around the fire. It showed them that Whirlwind might have been raised by white people, but that he had not really learned to be white at all. A blood vow of this sort was precisely what any of them would have made in similar circumstances. They invited Han to sleep around their fire that night, an offer which he gratefully accepted.

Han Jackson lay in the darkness thinking about his parents, both those who had raised him from his birth and the couple who had taken care of him for the last ten years or so.

While Han was thinking of Patrick and Esther Jackson, a man fifty miles away also had them on his mind. Tom Sweeney was sitting a space away from the others with his back to the fire, brooding about the turn events had taken in the last few months. He had picked up with the Holt brothers and found them exhilarating company for the first few weeks. It had gradually dawned on him though that there was something wrong with the pair of them. It was not that they were violent; Sweeney was himself no mean hand with a knife and gun and had killed more than one man with both weapons. The Holts though were in a class of their own.

When the five of them had fetched up at the Jacksons' farm, they had just been looking for a bit of cash money. The old man had been an awkward bastard and there was no denying it. He had made a run to the house, probably to fetch his gun, when Jed Holt had brought him down with a vicious blow to his head. Then he had dragged the old man to where Eli was holding his wife with a razor-sharp Bowie knife at her throat. Jed had told him that if he didn't tell them where his money was hid, then the old woman would get her throat cut. He had caved in at once and told them what they wanted to know. When one of the others had been sent off to the house and returned with a heap of gold coins, Sweeney thought that that was the end of it, that Eli and Jed would just turn the old folk loose and they would all ride off. Not a bit of it!

Jed nodded to Eli, who then slowly and deliberately cut the woman's throat. The blood gushed down the front of her dress and he could see the look of satisfaction in Eli's eyes as he watched the grief-stricken old man howling with anguish. Then Jed, who was still gripping the man fast from behind, shot him twice in the back and the old fellow fell dead next to his wife.

Tom Sweeney was not a squeamish man, but this cold-blooded killing almost caused him to protest. Almost, but not quite. He had a feeling that the Holts would not take kindly to anybody objecting to any course of action they saw fit to take or, for that matter, anybody bolting from their little team. So for now, he was staying with them, but only until he could see a safe way of getting clear and going back to working on his own.

While he was musing to himself along these lines, a hand suddenly clapped on to his shoulder. He reared in surprise, spilling his coffee and turning round fearfully to find Eli Holt looming above him. They might be right hefty-looking fellows, but both the Holt brothers could move as silently as rattlesnakes when they were minded to.

'What you doing sitting here alone, Sweeney?' enquired Holt jovially. 'You come and join the rest of us now. Unless you don't favour our company?'

'No, no, nothing of the kind. I's just thinking.'

'Thinking?' said Eli Holt, as though this was not an activity towards which he was well disposed, 'Thinking? You've no call to be exerting yourself in that direction, my friend.'

Sweeney stood up and went back to the fire with Eli. The other man laid his arm around Tom's shoulders in a friendly fashion, but it felt heavy and constricting to the frightened man, as though a large and dangerous animal had draped itself on his back with a view to ripping off his head.

When they got to the fire, Sweeney sat himself down and Eli caught his brother's eye. He made an imperceptible shake of his head, to which his brother responded with the slightest of nods. This exchange was unremarked upon by the other three men. The Holt brothers seldom had to speak out loud one to the other to lay their plans. They had both noted Tom Sweeney's reaction to the death of the Jacksons and now a death sentence had been passed upon him. If he did but know it, Tom Sweeney had less than twenty-four hours to live.

★ ★ ★

Han set out at dawn the next day. The party of dog soldiers were anxious to be off and about whatever business they had. They parted amiably from Han, wishing him well and invoking upon him the protection of Maheo, the supreme deity of the whole tribe. The others watched him ride south and then remarked in tones of great satisfaction that Hohanonivah had not learned as much of the white man's ways as one might think, even after spending ten years with them. Any one of them might have sworn a blood oath of that sort to avenge a relative's death.

Indeed, three of the party had already made similar vows, having like Han lost family members killed by the white men. There was no doubt in their minds that Whirlwind's spirit was unmistakably Cheyenne. With which reflection, they headed north to join the war against the bluecoats which was brewing up in Wyoming.

The encounter with the dog soldiers had cheered Han a little. His grief was none the less raw, but it had been good to have some human contact, the first since his parents' death. He rode hard that morning, interspersing long canters with spells of trotting. He ate in the saddle and then eased up on the pony a little after noon, allowing her to dawdle from time to time. There would be no purpose in laming the creature out here in the middle of nowhere.

When the afternoon was well advanced, Han saw in the distance a huddle of wooden buildings and soddies. It was no more than a hamlet by a stream, but it might be that he would hear news there of the men he sought. When he reached the place, he could see that although it numbered no more than two or three dozen buildings, it had a saloon of sorts. This was a low wooden building with a row of bottle affixed to the porch in order to indicate its function. This was a wise move in a district where the literacy rate was at that time running at around 0 per cent.

Inside, the place was smoky and dark. It was no more than a single, large room, with a few tables and an arrangement of planks at one end which served as a bar. A half-dozen men were sitting round; eating, drinking and talking in low voices. They all fell silent when Han entered the place. Although he did not realize the fact, he presented a strange and exotic figure to the inhabitants of the sleepy little hamlet, most of whom had in any case little reason to love Indians. As he walked towards the back of the place, looking for the owner, one of the men at the tables stood up and moved to intercept him.

'Redskins don't get served here, boy. We get enough trouble with you people without you getting liquored up and all.'

'I'm not looking for a drink. I'm not old enough, anyways.'

'You sassing me, boy?'

'No, sir,' said Han, still reasonable. 'I'm looking for some men who might have passed through this way.'

The man took Han's peaceful manner as weakness and felt encouraged to push him about a little. He shoved the young man in the chest, saying, 'Ah, get out of here, Injun!'

This would have been a bad mistake at the best of times, but getting crosswise to Hohanonivah less than twenty-four hours after he had been bereaved was really not the smartest move anybody could have made. He said nothing to the man in front of him; just stared at him appraisingly. Then, unexpectedly and with no warning at all, he clamped his right hand tight round the fellow's throat and ran him backwards towards the wall, knocking a chair over as he did so. The man's feet scrabbled for purchase, as he tried to avoid falling over. When they got to the wall, Han slammed the man into it hard enough to set his ears ringing. He plucked the pistol from the man's holster and threw it across the room. Then he drew his own piece with his free hand, cocking it with his thumb as he did so, and pointed it in the general direction of the other men in the room, one or two of whom had sprung to their feet.

There was no telling how matters might have developed if the owner of the joint, an elderly and good-natured man, had not come through from the back and sized up the situation pretty swiftly.

'Now then, now then,' he said affably, 'what are we all about here? Who started all this to-do?'

Han was surprised when one of the

men volunteered, 'It was Mike of course. He started twitting the Indian and then laid hands upon him.'

The barkeep tutted disapprovingly. 'I have done told you not once but many times, Mike Parker, you and me will be falling out if you keep up this habit of starting trouble in my place. And you, young man, you put up your weapon. I'll have no gunplay in here.'

Han released his grip upon the man's throat and then tucked the pistol back in his belt.

'That's more like it,' said the man behind the makeshift bar. 'Now, what can I do for you? Mind, I can't serve you with intoxicating liquor unless you are twenty-one years of age, which I would take oath is not the case.'

'I don't drink alcohol. I wouldn't put a thief in my mouth to steal away my brains.' Han was echoing his parents, who had been staunch Methodists and firm teetotallers. He had no idea how strange such words sounded, coming from the lips of an Indian.

'Yes, well,' said the owner of the saloon. 'What a mercy that most of the men around these parts are not of the same mind. Tell me, if you are not looking for a drink, what are you here for?'

'I'm looking for five men who might have ridden through here a couple of days since.'

There was a stirring of interest at this among the other customers. 'Well now, you don't say so?' said the barkeep. 'Five men, hey? Well, boys, what do you say? Can we help his young fellow?' There were grunts of assent. 'But first, maybe you could tell us what your interest in them is?'

'They killed my parents,' said Han flatly.

'Did they, by Godfrey? When was this?'

'I found them dead yesterday. Patrick and Esther Jackson, two of the best people that ever drew breath. It is my intention to find those who did this.'

'The Jacksons?' said the owner of the

bar thoughtfully. 'Might you be the boy that they took in after that dreadful business up at Sand Creek?'

'I am.'

'Well, if you'd said so earlier, it might have saved a little chasing round the woodpile, so to speak. I knew your parents years ago and I am right grieved to hear of their death. I heard that you were as devoted to them as if they was your own flesh and blood.'

'I was. Now I aim to bring the killers to justice.'

The old man pulled over a chair and invited Han to sit down, while he related the case to him and told what he knew of the men who had killed his folks.

★　★　★

While Hohanonivah Jackson was being furnished with fuller and further particulars of the men who had murdered his adoptive mother and father, those men themselves were

40

having a pretty lively time of it, not forty miles away.

Jed and Eli Holt, despite having committed such a dreadful crime, were feeling cheerful and relaxed as they and their band moved south earlier that day. It was fortunate that none of these men was given to either imagination or guilt and so their terrible actions seldom troubled them for long.

'Looks to me like we are heading for a pleasant time for the weather,' remarked Jed amiably to his brother.

'I've known worse,' said the other briefly. 'Ride on ahead with me now, I would have some few words alone with you.' Eli turned a cold eye on the others, saying, 'I know these fellows will not mind nor take it amiss.'

There were hasty nods of agreement and the men composed their faces into what they thought might be the look of those not in the least affronted or put out by the notion of the two brothers having a private conversation.

When they were out of earshot, Eli

said, 'I want rid of Tom Sweeney this very day, if it can be managed. He is setting the evil eye upon me and will bring us bad luck.'

Jed replied, 'We must wait for the right moment. I do not want to spook the others.'

'So be it.'

About the same time that Han Jackson was approaching the little settlement by the river, the Holt brothers and their accomplices were trotting south without being in any particular hurry. Tom Sweeney had been feeling uncomfortable ever since he had woken that day. He sensed a tension in the air, like you get sometimes before a thunderstorm.

Jed called out to his brother, 'Eli, what do you make to that?'

They all looked to where Jed had indicated. A body of men, perhaps fifteen or so, were heading towards them at a brisk trot. They seemed to be heading straight for them, but for what purpose, it was impossible to say. The five of them reined in and waited. They hadn't long to wait, because when the posse spotted them, they speeded up considerably and galloped towards the Holt brothers and their three companions.

3

There were fourteen men in the party which pulled up in front of the Holt gang. They formed a line, blocking the way in front of the other party of men. Only two of them had stars pinned to their shirts and one of these acted as the spokesman. 'Have you boys set eyes on two riders in the last few hours? Both young, one with a bloody bandage around his arm?'

'I cannot say that we have,' said Jed. 'Why, are you looking for them?'

'That we are,' said the sheriff grimly. 'You've not seen anybody?'

'Nary a one,' said Jed as pleasantly as could be. He could afford to be pleasant, it looking as though these men had no interest in them; which, by the by, was somewhat of a relief, seeing as how they outnumbered them three to one.

The whole episode might have passed off as quiet and peaceful as could be, with no bad feeling on either side, if the other man in the posse who was wearing a badge and who had been staring hard at Jed, hadn't announced loudly, 'You be Jed Holt and that there is your brother Eli. You are both wanted for murder!'

Some men at this point might have said words to the effect of, 'Surely, my friend, you must be mistaken!' or something similar. Others might have made a run for it, seeing that they were faced with overwhelming odds. Then again, there were those who might have surrendered with good grace and trusted in the judicial process to deal with the matter. It was at times such as these that the Holts came into their own. The words were scarcely out of the man's mouth and nobody had yet had a chance to digest them and weigh their import, when Jed Holt spurred his horse and rode straight at the man who had recognized him, drawing his pistol as he did so.

Just before he reached the line of men ahead of him, Jed Holt shot dead the man who had challenged him. He kept right on going and burst through the line and then wheeled round and began shooting some of the others in the back, before they had even realized what was happening. People sometimes remarked that the Holt brothers seemed like one single person at times like this. To anybody watching, it would have looked like Eli started riding forward at the self-same moment as his brother.

As Jed began shooting, so did Eli, only he took out the other man with a star first and also the man sitting next to him. Like his brother, he too broke through the line of men and then also started firing at them from behind. Their three followers took a while to get the drift of the thing and see where matters were tending, but when they did, they too drew their guns and began firing on the posse. Probably they realized that they would hang alongside the Holts if there were to be arrests and a trial following on from this affair.

All this furious activity was in full swing before any of the men in the posse even had a chance to think what was happening, never mind draw their own weapons. It was all one mad mêlée of shooting and confusion. As he rode back into the rear of the posse, Jed Holt caught a sight of Tom Sweeney with his gun in his hand, looking undecided as to what he should be doing next; whereupon Jed shot him dead, thus neatly solving the problem of being saddled with a weak and vacillating man who was likely to prove a liability in the future. This again was where the Holt brothers scored highly as successful bandits. Most men, they would have seen the gunfight with the fourteen armed men as a challenge; to Jed Holt, it had instead proved a welcome opportunity.

Now, incredible as it might seem to those who have not been mixed up in such goings on, none of the members of the posse had even yet started shooting. The explanantion was not hard to divine. Barring the sheriff and his regular deputy, who were now dead, they were all volunteers who had been sworn in and were riding like this for the few dollars that they would be paid as temporary deputies. Being shot at had not entered into their reckoning of the thing. Since they were most of them family men, the end result of the affair was not long in doubt. They feared to fire, as they did not all know each other by sight and so in the confusion and smoke of battle, they did not wish to shoot the wrong person. In short order, they every man-Jack of them cut and ran, leaving six of their number lying stone dead on the ground.

As the remaining eight members of the party galloped away, both Jed and Eli led out whoops of joy like

Comanche warriors and began discharging their guns into the air as a signal of triumph. The other two men could hardly believe that they were still alive. They had the both of them been in the thick of some lively adventures, but the way that the Holt brothers had behaved defied all belief. Still and all, they were alive and that was something to be thankful for.

There was some slight discussion about taking time to bury poor Tom Sweeney, but Eli, in a rare flash of humour, quoted the scriptural text about leaving the dead to bury the dead. His brother represented to them that it would surely not be long before those cowardly rascals returned to the scene in greater force and that the sooner they were all out of there the better. So Sweeney and the other six corpses were left out in the open, where later that night the coyotes made short work of them.

★ ★ ★

The bartender called one or two others over to tell Han about the men who had stayed the night in the saloon a couple of days previously. They had ridden in as the sun was fit to set and ordered food and drink. And they had paid in gold, which was not at all a common occurrence in that village. There had been some small debate about how to calculate the change from a ten-dollar gold piece, but after some wrangling, it was agreed that they would have as much as they pleased to drink on top of the food and the option to sleep on the floor there that night too, if so they wished.

The men had behaved courteously enough to the other customers of the place, even standing them drinks and inviting them to join the party. It was fairly plain that the travellers were about some sort of unlawful activity, but since they were doing no harm there, it did not much signify. They had not risen until almost noon on the next day and then made off south.

Between the bartender and the men who had been there that night, Han was able to build up a pretty comprehensive and accurate description of the men.

'My opinion to you, my boy,' said the owner of the little saloon, 'would be to leave those men to the duly constituted authorities, as one might say. I do not think that they are the kind of men that I would wish to try conclusions with.'

Han shrugged. 'I merely wish to show them that they should rather have troubled somebody other than my own family.'

There was silence. Although he had not stated his intention openly, it was not hard to divine his meaning. Not a man listening had any doubt that one way or another, murder would be done if this boy caught up with the men. This was a melancholy reflection, because he seemed a nice enough lad. Howsoever, he was not apt to be dissuaded from his purpose and since it was not really any affair of theirs, they bade him farewell. He declined

51

the offer of a bed for the night, giving it to be understood that he would carry on until the moon rose.

As he left the saloon, the man who had accosted him when first he entered, approached him and offered his hand. 'I hope we part well, young man? I had no business talking to you so and I am sorry for it.'

Han smiled at him. 'No hard feelings. I hope I did not hurt your head too badly.'

Mike Parker smiled a little ruefully. 'You have a powerful grip, fellow, and a strong arm behind it. I will live. Good luck.'

As he rode away from the little settlement, Han felt oddly cheered by the human warmth of the men he had met there. It reminded him that however much evil there might be in this world, it was always more than matched by the good. His parents had taught him this from the first day that he lived with them and they had lived their own humble lives according to this precept. He pictured them now, reading aloud from the Bible of an evening and explaining to the young boy that God loved the world and all people. Whether you called that god Jehovah or Maheo did not much matter to them; it was all one.

The sun had sunk below the horizon, but the moon had not yet risen. It was a good time to be out and about like this. If only his mission had not been such a grim one, Hohanonivah would have rejoiced to ride through the wilderness in this wise. He did not stop to rest until it was full dark and he was worried that he would cause the pony to set foot in a prairie dog hole or some such misadventure. He slept fitfully until first light and then they were on their way again. As far as he could gauge, he could not be more than thirty or forty miles behind the men he was following.

★ ★ ★

53

When they had set off from Wyoming, the Holt brothers and their three chance companions were heading for New Mexico. They had been travelling due south, with this in mind, when they had had the little dispute with the sheriff and his men. Since some of those who fled would probably have marked this, it seemed to the Holts that the best thing to do would be to change tack and head in another direction. North was out of the question, which left east or west. The Rockies were not a tempting prospect, there being nothing much there to steal and few people to prey upon and so they turned south-east in the general direction of Texas.

Eli and Jed were both well aware that the killing of a sheriff and half-a-dozen deputies was apt to stir up somewhat of a hornets' nest and so they felt it wise to put a little space between them and the scene of the crime. There was, after all, a limit to how far even the most determined posses would pursue fugitives. Besides, they knew a little place near the Texas panhandle where they might hole up for a while until things had died down a little.

Han knew nothing of these developments and so kept going south as fast as he and the pony could manage. At about midday, just when the sun was at her highest, he ran into what at first he thought could be serious trouble. It was a band of armed men who, as soon as they spotted him, rode down on him and desired him to throw down his weapons. Leastways, they did this after first speaking to him as though he were a deaf idiot, enunciating every syllable slowly and loudly. 'Do you speak English?' asked the man who seemed to be in charge. It dawned on Han that they were treating him so because he was Indian. He replied in his best Sunday School manner,

'Yes, I am obliged to you, sir, my English is tolerably fair.'

The men looked more closely at him. 'Well,' said the leader, 'you just cast down that rifle and also the pistol in your belt. Nice and slow, now.'

'What do you want with my guns?'

'Never you mind. Just do as I bid you.'

Han slowly and reluctantly did as he had been told.

'And the bow.'

'It isn't even strung!' protested Han. Two of the men cocked rifles. He threw down his bow as well. The man who was doing all the talking looked back and observed,

'Here comes Jake. He'll know if this was one of them.'

An older man cantered up and after reining in, asked, 'What's to do?'

'This one of them?'

'Hell, no. You think I wouldn't have said if one of them was an Indian?'

There seemed to be a general relaxation at the news that Han had not been 'one of them'. 'Anybody want to tell me what this is all about?' he enquired.

The man who had first spoken to him said, 'A bunch of our friends and neighbours was attacked yesterday by five men. They started shooting without warning and six men I knew well were killed. You know anything about that?'

Han thought quickly, concealing his excitement by holding his face immobile in the approved Indian fashion. 'Tell me,' he asked, 'were they heading south?'

'They were.'

'Seems to me like they might have changed direction. I passed a party of five men this morning, heading north.' Han gave the descriptions that the men in the saloon had furnished him with.

The man Jake, who had evidently seen them yesterday, cried in excitement, 'That's them, for a bet! Heading north you say?'

Han nodded. He had already figured out the case in his head. Obviously, after a spree of murder like the one these men were talking of, the five men he was trailing would not be foolish enough to keep on the same path. They would not be heading back north where, for all they knew, the alarm would by now have been raised about the murder of his parents. West lay the Rockies and there was not much there to draw anybody unless they had some business on the other side of the mountains. Besides, these men were going south for a purpose. The most likely dodge would be for them to head east for a space and then carry on south to wherever it was they were going in the first place.

It would not do to let these men know any of this though, because Han wanted to be the one to catch up with the men, not see them hanged for a crime about which he cared little.

There were various impatient exclamations from the men surrounding him. They were obviously keen to go racing north and catch ahold of the men who had killed men known to them.

'Can I pick up my guns and bow now? Yon fellow has told you I had no part in this affair.'

'I reckon so,' said the leader of the band.

Han jumped down and picked up his belongings. He fitted the rifle into its place along the front of the saddle and swung himself up.

It was at that point that things started to go wrong. One of the men said to the others, 'How do we know that he's not one of those dog soldiers we hear tell of? He might be riding to war for aught we know!'

'It may be so,' said the leader slowly. 'Maybe we should hand him over to the army and see what they say about this.'

Han did not wait to hear any more of the debate. He spurred his pony on and took off east. There were shouts of surprise and cries of anger, following by a few stray shots sent in his direction, but none of the men seemed disposed to follow him. He kept riding, a surge of excitement coursing through his blood. He knew that he was on the right track and that the fools he had left behind were both too slow-witted to stop him and also dull enough to allow him to send them off on a snipe hunt. His exultation was cut short when one of the men, the better part of a mile behind him now, fired off a parting shot from his old musket, which might have first seen service in the Mexican war. It fired a ball rather than a rifle bullet and this caught Han a glancing blow on the side of his head. Its energy was almost expended at that range or it would have cracked his skull open. As it was, it felt like being swiped round the head with a hickory stick.

Han managed to stay in the saddle and even maintain his speed, but the sickening pain told him that he would need to rest up before long. He turned his head to look back and almost passed out from the bolt of agony which went through his head and down his neck. The men who had stopped him had forgotten him entirely by the look of it and were moving north.

The rest of the afternoon was a nightmare. Han's head was throbbing and his eyes kept blurring. If he looked sideways, he could see two images. He began to worry that the musket ball had done him a mischief. There was no question of galloping or cantering; he would never have been able to stay in the saddle. Instead, he let the pony trot at her own pace. Once she sensed that Hohanonivah was no longer minded to speed her along, she slowed from a trot to a walk, even stopping altogether from time to time to nibble at some appetizing-looking plants.

As the hours dragged by, Han knew that he would have to stop for a spell. He simply couldn't bring himself to dismount though. He knew what the men he was hunting looked like, he was pretty sure that he was travelling in the same direction as they and all the indications were that he was no more than a day or so behind them. In the end, the decision was taken out of his hands. The pony was dawdling along, taking full advantage of her master's sickness. They were approaching a log cabin on the edge of a pine wood, when Han suddenly tumbled off on to the ground and passed out entirely.

Eli and Jed Holt were in the meantime approaching the small town of Tribulation, which lay right on the edge of the Colorado territory. They had friends here, judging by what they had said to Rick Harkness and John Cartwright; the two men who had come down with them from Wyoming.

Rick and John had known each other for a year or two, having fallen in together during a robbery in Caspar. They were a fiddle-footed pair of young rogues, neither of them much over twenty years of age. They had carried out various thefts together; anything from beating up and robbing drunks at the back of saloons to holding up stagecoaches. Both had killed men and neither had been too shocked by the murder of the Jacksons. What was disturbing them was not so much the fact that both the Holt brothers were mad cut-throats, as that the two of them didn't seem too much concerned whether they lived or died. This *was* alarming, because Rick and John were both very fond of life and wished to continue enjoying it for as long as ever they might. Since they had been travelling south with the Holts, it was gradually dawning on them that while they might be pretty rough customers in their own way, they were as gentle and innocent as newborn babes in comparison with Eli and Jed.

Tribulation had been established near to a tributary of the North Canadian River, nigh to the border with Texas. Perhaps two or three hundred souls lived there. It was an out-of-the-way kind of place, reached by a road which didn't seem to lead anywheres in particular. What the town lived on would be hard to say at first sight. There was a blacksmith, a general store and and a saloon; all that you might expect to find in a little town like that. Beyond that, there didn't seem to be any trade or industry to support the residents. No farmed fields within a dozen miles, no visible means of support at all, as one might say. The place appeared in some sense to keep itself to itself. It was not on a stage route, there was no telegraph office and the nearest railroad line, the Atchison, Topeka and Santa Fe, passed maybe forty miles north of Tribulation.

There was no mystery to those who actually lived in the town about where the money came from: it was, in effect, a centre for gun-running and smuggling. Comancheros from New Mexico used the place a lot and it was a handy halfway point for moving all sorts of goods from one place to another. There was another similar kind of town away to the west, called Midway, which had been where the Holts had originally been heading.

There was a fair bit of activity in the town when the Holt brothers and their two friends rode in, because various troubles with restless Indians were coming to a head.

Suddenly and without any warning, Jed Holt reined in his horse and turned to Harkness and Cartwright, saying, 'You boys don't enquire what we are going for to do in this town?'

Cartwright shrugged, looking a little uncomfortable. 'Figured you and your brother would tell us in good time,' he said at length.

'You got that right,' said Jed, and continued, 'I may as well state the case now and be done with it, else you all will be asking a heap of foolish questions once we hit town and that won't answer for our purpose.'

'We ain't about to shoot off our mouths,' said Rick Harkness, a mite too pertly for Jed's taste, because he said in a soft voice, 'Don't take that tone with me, boy, or you and me will be falling out and I don't reckon we either of us want that. You likely know that the Cheyenne are on the warpath. Well, they know they aren't getting far with just bows and arrows and spears and such, so they need guns. That's where

Midway and Tribulation come into the picture, as you might say. They are both centres for the traffic of deadly weapons or what you boys perhaps call gun-running.'

'We're going to sell guns to the red man?' exclaimed Cartwright incautiously.

Eli glared at the boy, causing him to fall silent, and said, 'Just shut your mouth while my brother speaks.'

Jed went on, 'It is the Comancheros who sell the guns and they make a right heap of profit out of it too. We are going to relieve them of some of that profit. That is all that I will say on that matter now, but I tell you so that you know enough to keep quiet and not ask questions.'

Now although Eli and Jed had at first been heading for Midway, the fact that they had had to change direction and fetched up instead in Tribulation did not really alter their plans to any great extent. This was because they hoped to team up with a group of rootless wanderers and attack a caravan of Comancheros returning from having sold their guns. They were sure to be in possession of plenty of gold, that being the commodity which they most desired to obtain in their deals with their Kiowa and Comanche customers. It would be plain folly to launch an attack on a band of Comancheros who were operating out of the town where the Holts were themselves staying at the time and so the intention was to single out a group heading for Midway. If the Holt brothers had, as they originally intended, reached Midway, then the boot would have been altogether on the other foot and they would have been targeting a band moving towards Tribulation. To this extent, their diversion did not matter at all and their plans remained unaltered.

'Jed, Eli,' cried the swarthy-looking owner of the larger of Tribulation's two saloons, when the four of them entered, 'where have you bastards been hiding for the last year? Things have got too hot for you, is that the case of it? You come here to hide out for a space, no?'

All this talking of things being hot for them and hiding out was a little too near the knuckle for the liking of the Holts.

'Raul, you have a mighty big mouth on you,' said Eli. 'Take care that one day you do not open it too wide.'

The other man laughed. 'Ah then, I am right? You are, how do they say, 'on the run', no?'

'Just give us some whiskey, you talkative cow's son,' said Jed Holt.

There were not many men in the place, seeing as it was not yet evening, just a handful of loafers, none of whom looked too dangerous. The Holts led their young friends over to a table in the corner of the room and then revealed their plans. The two boys listened carefully. It all sounded as safe and easy as a stroll in a pleasure garden to hear Eli and his brother describe things. They would recruit one or two likely fellows here and then ride down on a party of Comancheros who had just finished their business with the Indians. They would be sure to have a fair sum of gold about them, which only needed to be removed. The best bit of it was that there would be no trouble with the law after this exercise. Gunrunners are hardly going to scoot off to the nearest sheriff and complain that they have been robbed.

'You sure 'bout all this?' asked young Rick.

'You calling me a liar?' responded Eli in a deadly soft voice. Rick looked alarmed, until Eli and Jed both burst out laughing.

Later that night, the Holts met up with a few men who they seemed to know slightly and it was more or less agreed that in three days, they would ride down into New Mexico and lay an ambush for a group of men who were heading for Midway.

4

When Han came to, he couldn't quite figure where he was. It looked like a cave at first: gloomy and dark, with a low roof. After a spell he recollected that he had fallen from his pony near to a log cabin. The occupant of the cabin, or so he assumed, was standing by a little stove, humming a melancholy tune to herself. When she turned towards him, Han was surprised to see that it was an old black woman. There were few blacks living around that part of Colorado and so the sight of her was somewhat of a novelty to him.

'How are you feeling now, son?' the old woman asked.

'My head's sore, but except for that I will do, I guess. My pony . . . ?'

'I tethered her up. She is fine.'

'Thank you, ma'am.'

'Never mind 'ma'am'. My name is

Cassandra, but most everybody call me Cassie or Mama Cassie. Cassie will do.'

'I am right sorry to put you to this trouble.'

'Caring for a fellow being is no sort of trouble, son. It is what we are here on earth for. Do not set your mind further to it.'

'How long was I out for?'

'I don't measure time by hours out here. When you fell off your pony there, the sun was still high in the sky, but it has been set a good time since.'

'I have to be going. I am following some people and do not want them to esca — get too far a head of me. I am obliged for you help, but now I must go.'

'Who are you following? Friends, or the other thing?'

'It does not matter. I am in a hurry.'

'You climb up on that pony right now and you going to fall off again directly. Maybe not at once, perhaps when you are five miles down the track and there is no Mama Cassie to pick you up again. You must rest here at least tonight.'

'You don't understand. I have urgent business with some men. I must not let them get too far ahead of me.'

'What is this business?'

There was something so soothing and kind about the old woman, that Hohanonivah found himself telling her the story of his parents' murder. She listended quietly, without interrupting him; except once or twice telling him to slow down so she could get the matter straight in her mind. After he had finished speaking, she remained silent for a few minutes, before asking, 'And what is so urgent now? Why are you in such a hurry to catch up with the men who killed your folks?'

'I told you, I mean to give my parents justice.'

'Which I suppose in plain language means that you will kill those five men. Is that what your ma and pa would have had? Were they ones for revenge and murder?'

Han said nothing. The words summed up what had been tickling away at the back of his mind. Deep inside, he knew that his parents would have been horrified at the idea of a quest for vengeance of this sort. The old woman apparently guessed what was going through his mind. She stood up and went over to the table. On it lay a big, heavy Bible, like the one his parents had read from each and every evening. She opened it and read aloud, 'Vengeance is mine, sayeth the Lord; I will repay.' She closed the book and asked, 'Ain't that about the case here?'

Han said nothing. She was, of course, right, and deep in his heart he knew that the road he was on would not be what his adopted mother and father would have been pleased to see. He turned his head restlessly. His neck still felt sore, but the double vision had gone. He sat up and swung his legs over the side of the bed upon which he had been laid.

'Say,' he said, 'how did you get me in

here and up on this bed? I must be twice your size.'

Mama Cassie chuckled. 'I was a slave for nigh on fifty years. We was worked hard in the fields and I reckon the muscles I made in those days have not gone.'

'You remind me of my parents. They worked their farm until they were over seventy. My pa, he could still harness up the horse and plough a field quicker than many a man half his age.'

The old woman nodded. 'Yes, that's the way of it. Those that grow old and feeble oft times set out to do so. I do not have the inclination to be a helpless old woman.'

Han stood up and was encouraged to note that he did not feel sick any more. Cassie eyed him disapprovingly. 'You are determined then to follow the same road you was on when I found you?'

He looked at her seriously. 'I will take heed of what you have said. You are right: I was not raised to this and I do not think that those good people would

74

have wished me to do murder on their behalf. I need though to know what would make a man kill such a harmless pair of old people. I owe them that.'

Mama Cassie stared at him thoughtfully for a few seconds. 'If you are minded to continue your journey, then there is nothing I can do to stop you. I can guess where you will find the men you seek. There is a little town south east of here. It is called Tribulation. All the bad people hereabouts tend to end up there. I think that you will find what you are looking for there, although perhaps you will not care for it when you find it.'

'Thank you for your help. I hope that we will meet again.'

'It may be, young man, it may be. God bless you.'

* * *

Rick and John were not being comforted by any kind, old, wise woman. Instead, they were feeling tormented by

75

a nameless fear. The Good Book says that, 'The wicked flee where none pursueth.' This was about what those two young men were feeling around the time that Hohanonivah Jackson was taking his leave of the old woman who had taken care of him.

They did not know anybody in Tribulation and so felt a little out of their place to begin with. This feeling was made a sight worse by the fact that just about everybody seemed to know the Holt brothers. Had they been a little older and more observant, they might perhaps have noticed that much of the friendliness shown towards Eli and Jed Holt was forced, and motivated less by a desire for their company than a fear of offending them by refusing a drink or declining to join them at their table. Nobody particularly wanted to get crosswise to the Holts or to give them cause to think that they were at outs with them.

However much they drank, neither of the Holts ever looked to be much the worse for wear. They remained as sharp-eyed and mean in their cups as when they were stone-cold sober. One of the things that both Rick and John had observed was that the Holts did not like to think that the two boys were going off together. Maybe it made them think that a conspiracy was being hatched against them. Fact is, they had not had a single moment since leaving Wyoming when the two of them were together without at least one of the Holts being in earshot. This had all happened so naturally, that neither of the boys had marked it.

That night in the saloon in Tribulation, there were so many people crowded round the Holts, that even they could not keep track of everybody. When Rick went out back to make water, John took the opportunity to follow him out. The two of them stood there companionably, pissing out into the darkness. As they fastened up their pants, John asked his friend, 'What do you think to this here, Rick?'

Instinctively, Rick looked round to see if one of the Holts might be listening. Being assured that they were alone, he replied cautiously, 'What do you mean, like?'

'I mean all this business with us riding along of Eli and Jed.'

There was a pause, before Rick said hesitantly, 'I mind that we had more fun when it was just the two of us. Not that I am saying anything against the Holts. Life just strikes me as less fun lately, is all.'

'You mean,' said John, 'like we are afeared, which has not been the case before we teamed up with the Holts.'

'That is the strength of it. I never relax, but that one of them is not watching me. I am uneasy in my mind at times.'

'What do you make of Tom Sweeney?'

'I don't make nothing of him: he's dead.'

'Do you think that he was shot by the posse?'

'That is a blazing strange question.

Who else might have killed him?'

'I do not believe that any of those men even fired their pieces. They cut and run too quick for that. It was only us doing the shooting.'

'You think that one of us shot him by accident?'

'No, I do not think that.'

At that moment, two other men came stumbling out and Rick and his friend went back inside. They were just in time to be furnished with new evidence that they had taken a wrong turning by hooking up with the Holt brothers.

It was necessary to be very careful around Eli and Jed at the best of times, but never more so than when they were liquored up. It was then that they were at their most unpredictable and deadly. If they were smiling and laughing, then you'd better be damned sure that you were smiling too, otherwise one of them would be apt to accuse you of not enjoying their company. If they were sober and straight-faced, then they were liable to resent anybody who looked like he might be having a good time. Trouble was, they could switch from one mood to the other in the blinking of an eye. One minute everybody would be laughing and joshing one another, and the next, one of the brothers was after killing a man for some fancied slight. Which was just exactly what was going on when Rick and John rejoined the crowd surrounding Eli and Jed.

Everything had been just fine and dandy, with the Holts in the best of moods. Somebody offered to top up Jed's glass and he placed his hand over the glass, declining. A man on the fringe of the group had joked, 'What's the matter, fellow, can't hold your liquor?'

Jed had turned cold eyes upon the offending man, the smile leaving his face in an instant. 'What was that, you whore's son?' he enquired, in a low and menacing voice. Conversation stopped in the group and the bonhomie swiftly evaporated. The chilly silence spread outwards from the Holts' table to the rest of the saloon, until the whole place was quiet. The man who had made the unguarded remark tried to backtrack.

'Hey, I didn't mean nothing by it. I was only joshing!' He flashed a sickly smile at Jed Holt, which only had the effect of angering that man all the more.

'Don't you grin at me like a damned baboon, you hear what I tell you? What was it you said about me, tending towards the line that I am not able to drink like a man?'

'Hey, I didn't say nothing like that — ' he began, when Eli cut in right fast.

'Why, are you calling my brother a liar?'

Jed got to his feet slowly. 'We had best settle this outside,' he said, measuring up the other man thoughtfully as though wondering what size he would take in coffins. The man who had made the foolish joke could hardly believe what was happening. Only a minute since and he had been on the best of terms with two double-dyed villains and been rehearsing in his mind the story that he would tell his wife the next day of how he had sat drinking all night with the Holt brothers. Now, he was all but a dead man. As he stood up, he kept expecting Jed and Eli to start laughing and tell him that this had been one of those crazy games of theirs. They did nothing of the sort.

Generally an episode of this sort is likely to end in nothing worse than a black eye or knocked-out tooth. Howsoever, when all the parties involved are armed to the teeth, then the consequences might be a good deal more tragic than that. Den Sothill, the man who had upset Jed Holt, was carrying a gun on his hip; more as a show-off stunt while drinking in the saloon than because he was the kind of person to start shooting anybody. In fact he carried lumber into town in his wagon and was not the type to get embroiled in rough-housing and gunplay. If Jed knew this, then it made no odds to him.

He felt insulted and was going to make it known to all in Tribulation what would be the likely result of getting crosswise to him.

The two men walked out into the dark street outside the saloon. The moon was shining bright, it was a Comanche Moon, that is to say full as could be, and this gave the scene an eerie beauty. Sothill could hardly walk, he was that frightened. He still entertained the faint and remote hope that the business would pass off peaceably and it would turn out that the Holt brothers were just fooling around to scare him. He took a stand a few yards along the street, facing where Jed Holt was watching him like a cat.

'Eli,' called Jed to his brother, 'you count to three now, and me and this son of a bitch will fire on three.'

Most of the folk in the saloon had followed the main characters in this little drama out into the street and the rest had their noses pressed to the window of the saloon. Den Sothill and

Jed were facing each other about thirty feet apart.

'One,' said Eli in a loud voice. Sothill tried in vain to still the trembling in his legs. He stamped his foot angrily and realized that he had an overwhelming urge to make water.

'Two.' Jed looked to have recovered his good humour and he was eyeing Sothill with a half smile on his lips. Maybe, thought Sothill, he had been right and this was all just some mad game to the Holts.

'Three!' Neither man made any move. Sothill almost fainted with relief as he realized that he had not been shot after all.

'Are you going to pull that pistol?' enquired Jed Holt, 'or do I have to come over there and start slapping you around?'

Everything somehow became sharp and clear to Sothill at that moment and he knew that he would either have to kill this bully or be shamed forever, maybe worse. He reached for his gun and then fired towards Holt. The other man did not move a muscle. There was something terrifying about the way that Holt simply stood there, apparently perfectly at ease while being used for target practice in this way. It was almost more frightening than if Jed Holt had been blustering and firing back at him. Instead, he just remained perfectly still, like he didn't have a care in the world and was happy for Den Sothill to fire away at him to his heart's content.

Sothill fired again and missed a second time. He felt as though he was in some kind of waking nightmare. He took more careful aim and that was when Jed Holt drew his gun and shot Den Sothill right in the eye, blowing off the back of his head. He holstered his gun and strolled back into the saloon. His brother clapped him on the back, saying, 'Nice work.'

5

The moon had risen and Han was wondering why in hell he hadn't accepted the old woman's offer of hospitality for the night. Deep inside, he knew the answer: it was that if he had let her talk to him for much longer about the foolishness of revenge, he might have turned round and headed home again the next morning. It is, after all, always irritating to be told something that you already know inside of you. It can be aggravating and makes you sometimes want to get away from the person who is giving the wise advice that you are resolved not to heed. So it was with Han. The sooner he parted company with Mama Cassie, the easier he would find it to hold to his purpose.

Still and all, by the time that Han had got eight or ten miles along the track alongside the pine wood, he had come to what almost amounted to a decision. It was this: he might very well not follow through on his plan to wreak vengeance on the men who had killed his parents. His head was throbbing again, which made clear thought hard and if there was one thing he knew, it was that it is a bad idea to make important decisions late at night. His ma and pa had quoted the scriptural text to him often enough about morning bringing counsel. In other words, first get a good night's sleep and then see how the case appears in the bright light of day. He accordingly camped up on the edge of the wood and fell asleep almost immediately.

The next day, things were a lot clearer in Hohanonivah's mind. He was sure as he gnawed a hunk of bread and cheese that Mama Cassie had been right, *was* right about the road he was on. He had set out in hot blood and either he would succeed and have murder on his conscience, or he would fail and lose his life. Looked at in the light of a bright clear morning, neither option looked precisely wonderful. He decided that he would turn back and talk things over with the old woman. Maybe she could help him to see things a little clearer. There was that about her anyways which reminded him of his adopted mother. It would be a pleasure to talk about his grief and suchlike. He had an idea that she would make a mighty good listener.

Han had barely got this plan straight in his head, when circumstances conspired to upset it. Although he had lit no fire himself that morning on rising, he was aware of the tang of woodsmoke in the air, not too close, but not a hundred miles away neither. He had mounted his pony and was turning her head to go back along the way he had come when a group of three horses emerged from the wood by which he had camped. They were sturdy little Indian ponies and on two of them sat a couple of proud-looking young men, Kiowa by the look of them. On the third was a white man, trussed like a fowl and laid across the saddle of the third pony like an animal, laid on his stomach with his hands and feet roped under the animal's belly.

He didn't know what the game was, but Han did not like the look of this one little bit. The two Indians had reined in and were staring at him suspiciously. Han rode forward and when the man heard another horse, he commenced screaming for help.

'Help me! These men have killed my family and taken me prisoner.' The voice was too high for a man, and when Han looked closely, he saw that the person was actually a girl dressed in a shirt and pants. When she saw that Han was also an Indian, she stopped shouting, presumably taking it for granted that he too was a Kiowa and probably in league with those who had captured her. The two other men sat there, motionless and impassive, waiting to see what Han would do.

'I think that you should let her go,'

declared Hohanonivah in English. The men made no move, but continued to stare at him. He repeated what he had said in Cheyenne. This time, they laughed. They probably didn't speak all that much Cheyenne, but they understood enough to grasp what he was saying.

The sight of that girl tied up like a hog meant that Han was not about to ride away from this encounter. He would not have been able to live with himself. Very slowly, he drew out his knife, which was as sharp as a razor and almost nine inches long. He threw it to the ground, where it stuck in the sod between his pony and that of the others. They, like he, had rifles as well and there was no real reason why either of them should have accepted a challenge of this sort. Nevertheless, one of the men took out his own knife and flung it down next to Han's.

The two of them dismounted, neither taking his eyes from the other for a moment. Han and the Kiowa picked up their knives and began to circle each other, looking for an opening. Nothing had been further from his mind when he woke up that morning than doing any manner of hurt to a fellow being, but he could not ride off and leave that girl. Not if he was to remain a man and be able to look the rest of the world in the eye.

The Kiowa made the first move, jumping at Han and clutching at his shoulder. Before he was able to follow this up by thrusting with his knife, Han hooked his leg round the other man's knee and brought him to the ground. At this point, he should have leapt upon the prone figure and stabbed him mercilessly, but he found that he just couldn't do it. Instead, as though this had been a kid's fight in the schoolyard, he backed off and allowed the Kiowa brave to get to his feet. There was a gleam of satisfaction in the man's eyes. He knew that he was dealing with a weakling who did not have the belly for a real fight. He was distinctly more jaunty now, moving forward as he swung his blade back and forth in front of him. It struck Han that if he was not careful, he was going to get himself killed this morning.

As Han retreated, so the Kiowa came on, obviously believing that it was only a matter of seconds now until he cut this impudent Cheyenne's throat. Han suddenly bent down and swept up a handful of the loamy soil, which he flung in his opponent's face. A lot of it went into the man's eyes, because he gave a bellow of anger and frustration. Han darted forward, past the other man and then picked up a large rock. Before the Kiowa brave knew what he was about, he lamped the man on the back of the head with the rock, knocking him senseless.

Having defeated his adversary, although admittedly in a somewhat unorthodox fashion, Han did not feel inclined to trust in the fellow's sense of fair play. He was right by his own pony and with one smooth, swift movement, he drew his rifle from the saddle, cocked it and said again in Cheyenne, 'Let her go.' The fellow glared murderously at Han, but saw that he would not be able to bring his own weapon to bear before Han got off his shot. Slowly and reluctantly, he dismounted and went over to the horse where the girl was being carried. He took out his knife and slashed at her bonds. She fell to the ground.

Han moved round a little, so that the girl was not in his line of fire if there was to be any shooting. The other man was still lying on the ground. He had not moved, but was making some strange snoring sounds. Han hoped that he was not going to die.

She was older than Han had guessed; probably not more than a year or so younger than he himself. When she stood up and began rubbing her wrists, she had the sense to move out of the way.

'Bring that pony round here,' he told her. 'Don't block my view of yon fellow while you are doing so.'

93

When the Kiowa realized that Han purposed to take the pony as well as the girl, he began speaking angrily in his own language. He couldn't rightly make out much of what the man was saying, beyond the fact that he thought that Han was violating some custom.

Han said in English, 'I can't help that, fellow. My pony cannot be expected to carry two people, not for long, anyways.' Keeping the man covered, Han went over and emptied both the Indians' rifles of cartridges, throwing them towards the trees. Then he bade the girl to get into the saddle so that they could be making tracks. All the while, he kept his rifle pointing towards the second Indian, who looked as though he would likely enough murder Han if the slightest opportunity were to present itself.

There now arose the question of which way to head. Han did not think that he could really bring any trouble down upon the head of Mama Cassie. If he made for her place, those fellows might trail him and that would be a poor return to her for her hospitality and help yesterday. Which meant that he would be best advised to continue on the trail away from her cabin. He said to the girl, 'You ride on ahead for a space. I will follow on, setting a watch on this man, who I deem to be wanting to shoot me. Can you ride fast when I give word?'

'This pony has no stirrups,' she replied.

'I do not wish to discuss his tack. Can you ride fast as he is?'

'I reckon so.'

Han let the girl get a lead of twenty-five yards and then slowly rode on himself, leaning back and keeping his rifle trained on the man whose pony he had stolen. He couldn't hold the gun to his shoulder, so simply kept the stock on his hip, so that at least the barrel was pointing in the right general direction. The man still had not moved. With a sudden, rapid jerk, Han returned the weapon to its scabbard and shouted,

'Ride!' to the girl.

Upon which, Han and the girl he had rescued spurred on their mounts and galloped away. Although he was fairly confident that the Indians would give it up as a bad job and not essay a pursuit, Han felt a curious tickling between his shoulder blades as they began riding off at speed. It was in the spot where he imagined a rifle bullet might strike him, if fired from behind by an angry warrior.

* * *

In Tribulation, people were discussing the previous night's shooting. Under their breath, they muttered that those Holt brothers were a pair of bastards and that Den Sothill had been a good man. To Eli and Jed's faces though, they were all smiles and affability. Truth to tell, shootings of this nature were not an uncommon occurrence in the town. There was a sheriff, but he had long since sold his soul to the gunrunners and turned a blind eye to most of the crimes that were committed in Tribulation. In this case, he was on solid ground, because all the witnesses agreed that Sothill had fired the first shot; had in fact fired twice at Jed Holt before the other man had fired back. It was an open and shut case of self-defence.

The plan was that the Holts, along with Rick, John and a few other people that they had recruited, would ride across into New Mexico and scout out the road that day upon which they wished to set their ambush. Word was that the men in whom they had an interest would be riding west along this road, heading for Midway, the next day at about noon. By means that they did not vouchsafe to share with the others, the Holts had established to their own satisfaction that the men whom they would be jumping would have a store of gold in their possession. They would be keeping some as their legitimate profits and investing the rest in another consignment of Winchesters which they would sell on to either the Comanches or Cheyenne, depending upon who had the most money to spend.

The seven men rode out of Tribulation in the late morning, heading west first and only changing direction and turning south once they were out of sight of the town. The road lay fifteen miles away, and it was perfect for an operation of this kind. There were rocks to hide behind, trees to provide shelter and, best of all, the place was remote and any gunfire was unlikely to attract attention. From what the Holts had said, there would be a wagon with six, maybe seven or eight riders accompanying it. These men might be hard, but the intention was not to engage them in any sort of equal match. Rather, they would fire on them from cover without any warning and with a little good fortune, most of the men would be killed before they even knew that they were under attack.

They broke their fast at the spot

chosen for the ambush and then smoked a little. Three of the men played a desultory game of cards for broken twigs, while Eli and and Jed went off out of earshot to talk over their ideas. This was always how the Holts worked. They decided what was what and then those around them fitted into their plans.

* * *

After Han was tolerably sure that they were not being pursued by the Indians whose pony they had stolen, he allowed that it would be all right to slow down to a trot for a while. He felt that he might appear uncouth for not having previously introduced himself, notwithstanding that the circumstances had been so tense. He told the girl, 'My name is Han Jackson.' She looked at him doubtfully.

'You don't talk like an Indian,' was her remark. Han was annoyed.

'You mean I don't whoop and holler

like a Comanche on the attack? You are right. I would venture to say that I speak English as well as you though.'

'I'm sorry. Don't take on, I didn't mean to offend you. It just sounds kind of strange, hearing an Indian speak so.'

'You say that those men killed your family. I am sorry.'

'Oh, they weren't real family. I mean they were, but not like my ma or pa. They been dead these ten years or more. No, it was some sort of cousins I lived with. They did not much care for me and I worked harder than a slave for them.'

'Still and all, it must be a grief to you that they are dead.'

'I will survive. By which I mean that I *have* survived, thanks to you. My name is Betty Lou. Just call me Betty or Bet, as the mood takes you.'

Han said nothing for a while and then asked, 'Tell me, Betty, where does this road take us?'

'It leads on to Tribulation. Which sounds like something out of scripture, but that is what the town is really called.'

'I have heard of this place. Can you tell me about it?'

Betty was looking over to the left, where grey-blue woodsmoke trickled up into the sky. 'Yonder was the farmhouse where I lived,' she said casually.

'Do you want to go there?'

'Go there? To what purpose?'

'I don't know. To collect your things maybe?'

'I didn't own much. What little I had was burned up when they torched the house. I have only what you see.'

'Do you want us to bury your relatives?'

'I am not fussed,' said Betty. 'It is nothing to me.'

Han was a little shocked at the callous way that the girl talked. He tried to excuse it to himself by making allowance for the shock which she had had that day. He was not best pleased to find himself going to Tribulation despite his change of mind that morning. He could not just leave this girl out here. He supposed that at the very least he would have to see her safe into town and then he would be able to turn right round and go back to see Mama Cassie. That is, he thought to himself, unless those Indians I tangled with are waiting for me on the road. Things have not turned out today as I could have wished them to, not by a long sight.

* * *

The Holts and their gang were making their way back to town, everything looking like it would be an easy piece of work on the morrow. The main thing would be to make sure that they gave no warning before opening fire on the Comancheros. That the success of this whole, entire enterprise depended upon the murder of eight or ten people did not trouble the conscience of any of the seven men who were riding back towards Tribulation.

Of a sudden, Eli said, 'You boys been mighty silent today. I hope you are not turning yellow or nothing of that kind?'

If it had been most anybody else in the world apart from one of the Holt brothers asking a question of that nature to Rick and John, then there would have been blood spilled and no mistake. There are those people in the world though whom we are disposed to resent when they accuse us of cowardice, and there are also those to whom we will allow this liberty. The Holts belonged in this second category and so neither Rick nor John showed any outward sign of anger.

'You don't need to think that,' said John shortly. 'You have seen me in action. I don't shrink from doing what is needful.'

Eli gave the impression of being dubious still. 'I am afeared that you and your friend might let us down. I did not observe you to be too lively when we crossed that posse just recently.'

This was too much for Rick, who cut

in, 'I shot a man and so did John here. I am not one to bolt when lead starts flying.'

John tried to signal his friend to stop, which gesture was noticed by Jed.

'Yes,' said Jed, 'you would do well to take heed of what your partner is indicating to you. My brother and me do not take overmuch to those who argue with us.'

The other three men viewed this exchange as some species of private quarrel between the Holts and the other two. They kept their own counsel and watched to see how matters would pan out. It looked both to them and also to the two boys, the Holts were trying to provoke a confrontation like that which had taken place the previous night.

In the event, nothing came of it. Eli rode right up close to John and slapped him hard on the back. 'Ah, you jumpy bastard, you think I was going to pick a fight with you?' Since that was just exactly what John had been thinking, he decided to say nothing and treat the whole thing as a joke. Later on though, he caught Rick's eye and he had the idea that Rick was thinking the same as him, namely how long it would be before the Holts really did set out to begin a fight and they found themselves served in the same way as the late Den Sothill. The ride back to Tribulation was pretty quiet after this, with nobody wanting to aggravate the Holts by saying anything out of turn which might be interpreted as an insult or challenge.

★　★　★

Betty seemed to want to chat as they travelled along. 'How come you speak such good English?' she asked curiously after they had moved past the burnt-out farmhouse.

'I was raised by white folks,' said Han, a little ashamed to refer to his ma and pa in this vague way.

'You don't say so? I have heard tell of

such things, but never met one like you in the life. Do you remember living with the Indians when you was little?'

'How come you were staying with your cousins? It sounds like the same sort of case to me.'

'Don't you want to talk about your real family? Why is that?'

Han did not reply. He saw no need to give her chapter and verse about his early life and in any case he preferred riding alone in general and did not like talking while in the saddle.

Betty could not keep quiet for more than a few minutes and was impervious to snubs. 'Are you vexed with me? You are not saying much.'

'How far would you say it is to Tribulation? Are we apt to arrive before nightfall?'

The girl shrugged indifferently. 'I don't know. I hardly ever went there. My folks had too much work for me to do on the farm. Like I say, they treated me worse than a slave.'

It was a glorious morning and Han's

only regret was that he was stuck with this talkative girl and not able to enjoy being out on his pony like this. Every so often, he cast a glance back, half expecting to see the two Kiowa come riding down on him, but there was no sign of them. After he had looked back anxiously for the twentieth time, Betty said, 'Are you worried about those other Indians? Are you afeared that they will come after us?'

'The thought had crossed my mind. You do not seem to have been much affected by the ordeal which you underwent. How is that?'

She laughed. 'Oh, I am what you might term adaptable. Riding a pony like this sure beats being slung over it like a tied hog. I am just glad that things have improved for me is all. You think I am cold-hearted for not grieving after my dead relatives. I guess you are right.'

The problem was that Hohanonivah Jackson had not had many dealings with girls in his life and so had no way of knowing if this one were especially flighty and annoying or if the whole breed were like that. Either way, he was counting the minutes until he could get to Tribulation, dump her there and return to spend a good long while talking to Mama Cassie.

⋆   ⋆   ⋆

Although none of the men who were planning on riding with the Holt brothers the next day said so in so many words one to the other, they were all of them a little wary about the whole set-up. On the face of it, it all sounded just fine. With luck, they would each take at least a couple of hundred dollars in gold for a half-hour's work and the way that Eli and Jed set the expedition out before them, there was little or no risk. They would be seven against eight or ten and they would have the advantage in that they would be firing from cover and taking the other band by complete and utter surprise. Even so, everybody other than the Holts themselves was getting a little nervous.

As darkness fell, the saloon began to fill up with various ghoulish types who wished to catch a sight of the famous Holt brothers who had gunned down one of their neighbours the night before. Eli and Jed wanted to drink and so those who would be riding by their side the next day were more or less obliged to sit with them and favour them with their company. It would have been a risky undertaking to look as though any of them were spurning the brothers' company that night. You just never knew where you were with the Holts. Mistaking their mood might earn you a scowl, a laugh or, as had been seen the previous day, sudden, bloody death.

6

Han and the girl made it into Tribulation by dusk. He still had the two gold pieces and so tried to book them rooms at a little boarding house to which a passer-by directed him. He surely needed a wash. He also needed to work out how to break free of Betty. As if all that were not enough, there was an excellent chance that the men who murdered his parents were present in this very town and although he had more or less foresworn vengeance after speaking to Cassie, he would rather not put this to the test by coming face to face with the bastards.

When Han offered one of the ten-dollar pieces to the owner of the boarding-house, the woman gave him an odd look and said, 'Well, I declare, this is a strange coincidence. Somebody over at the saloon tried to change one of these just yesterday. You do not often see them hereabouts. Are you something to do with the fellows staying at the saloon?'

'I am not,' said Han curtly.

'We don't generally get many of your type staying in town, meaning no offence,' said the woman. 'They mostly tends to stay out of town and sleep the Lord knows where, only coming in during the daytime. Meaning Indians, that is to say. You will not mind me asking if you have any peculiar habits?'

'Peculiar habits?' asked Han, confused.

'Well, I mean you will not be wanting to dance or chant, or anything tending in that direction? Only I have other guests to think of.'

'I will only be washing myself and sleeping in the bed. I hope that that is acceptable?'

'Lord, don't take on. I have to ask. We have had Mexicans stay here before now and you would not want to hear about the state that they left the room.

This place may not be much, but it is my livelihood.'

Betty chipped in at this point. 'I hope my room faces south? I cannot sleep in any other sort.'

The boarding-house owner did not look as though she had taken to young Betty. She gave her a sour look and said, 'I couldn't say what compass point the window in your room faces. If it don't suit, there is always the saloon. They, too, rent rooms.'

Han cut in to smooth things over, 'I am sure that both the rooms will be just fine. Thank you. My friend is not used to fine places such as this and so she is, as you might say, overawed.'

The woman was mollified by this, remarking, 'Well *some* people have good enough manners, I will allow.'

As they climbed the stairs, the girl said angrily to Han, 'What are you talking of fine places for? I have seen cleaner kennels than this.'

'That is as may be, but I wish to sleep in a bed tonight. I have not been in a bed for over a week now.'

Betty stopped dead. 'Where are you heading for? I forgot to ask. And I also forgot to thank you for rescuing me from those Indians, which was not grateful of me. If not for you, then the good Lord alone knows what would have befallen me.'

'I have no doubt,' said Han, 'that you would have survived well enough, whatever happened.'

She chuckled at that. 'Well that may be true. I have done all right today at any rate.'

★   ★   ★

Over at the saloon, there was not what one could call a cheerful atmosphere. Many of those who had drifted in to catch a sight of the notorious Holts had soon drifted out again. Nobody wanted to be the next person to whom the brothers took exception. This was the problem with Eli and Jed. They were pretty free spenders and they often attracted a crowd of hangers-on who also spent a fair bit. At times like this though, when they were just sitting there, staring into space moodily and tapping their feet, anybody with a grain of sense or any instinct for self-preservation took one look at them and then turned back out the door to go somewhere else.

Tonight, it was just the two brothers and their five followers, all clustered round a couple of tables. Other people drinking there were keeping as far as they could from the Holts' table; you might have thought they had some contagious disease. If Eli and Jed noticed this, they weren't giving any sign of it. After a time, when they had taken a few more whiskies, they began to loosen up a bit and everybody in the place breathed a sigh of relief. It was around this time that a young Indian strolled into the place, ordered a glass of buttermilk and sat down at a table not all that far from the Holts and their cronies. This was when things took an unexpected turn.

While they were getting liquored up, the Holts liked to relive what they saw as their triumphs: events surrounding their actions which led to the injury or death of some hapless man or woman. By great ill fortune, Eli was now boasting to his new companions about how he had robbed Han's parents. Now, even when they were drunk and in a pretty safe spot like Tribulation, the Holts stopped short of openly bragging about murder, but they found the scene when Patrick and Esther Jackson had each been pleading with them to spare the other, irresistibly comic. Eli put on a falsetto voice, supposedly like that of an old woman.

'Don't you tell 'em nothing, Patrick. I ain't afeared of these here brigands.'

Then he was Patrick Jackson, with a gruffer voice. 'Now you leave her be! Don't you harm a hair on her head, I'll fetch you out our gold. Will you leave us then?'

Jed roared with laughter at this little

bit of burlesque. Then his eyes lit on the Indian who was sitting at a nearby table, as immobile as a statue and looking straight at him and his brother like they were a pair of mangy dogs which had wandered in.

'What the hell are you looking at, you damned savage? And, come to the point, what are you doing in a saloon anyways?'

Han remained perfectly still and did not allow his face to show a trace of the loathing and disgust that he was experiencing. He had his pa's pistol tucked into his belt and the temptation to pull it out now and shoot down the man who had been mocking his parents was almost overwhelming. He had not the slightest doubt that at that table were the men who had killed his ma and pa and were now jeering about them, like they were nothing. He gazed steadily into Jed Holt's eyes.

'Can you hear me, boy?' said Jed loudly. 'Hey, you shit-head, I'm talking to you. What's the matter, don't you speak English?'

And still Hohanonivah Jackson just sat at the table looking at Jed Holt like he was watching a crawling snake to which he didn't care to get too close. Jed lurched to his feet, almost overturning the table as he did so. Han also stood up and walked out from the table to see what this braggart and bully would do next. The man might have been able to push around his ma and pa, who were in their seventies, but Han thought that he was in for something of a shock if he thought that he could play the same game with him.

Jed evidently did think just exactly that, because he walked slowly and menacingly towards Han, plainly hoping to scare him into backing away. The saloon was that still you could literally have heard a pin drop if somebody had chanced to drop one. After the previous night's affair, folk sitting there that night would not have bet a nickel on the young Indian's chances of living until the next morning.

The two men were now standing face to face, no more than two feet apart. One of them had to make a move and it was Han. He thought about this man laughing at his companion's jokes about Han's dead parents. He had no doubt that he and the one who had been impersonating them had both had a hand in their murder.

It happened so fast that in that smoky and gloomy room, if you had blinked your eye, you would have missed it. Han pulled the pistol from his belt, cocking it with his thumb as he did so. At the same moment, he grabbed Jed Holt's shirtfront and pulled him forward so that their faces were almost touching. Han rammed the barrel of the Colt right up into Jed's jaw, so that it forced back his head to one side. They stood there for a second or two like that; so close together that they could have kissed.

For a short space of time, Holt's life hung there in the balance. It wasn't until that point, when he had Holt at his mercy, that Han realized that he couldn't shoot a man in cold blood. Whatever vows he had made on the grave of his parents and leaving aside what Mama Cassie had said to him, he just plain could not do it. He was not a cold-blooded killer. It was a close thing though and Holt knew it. What Han marked later when thinking over the incident was the expression on the man's face. He was excited. He was perfectly aware that for some reason he couldn't fathom, this Indian might be about to blow his head off, but instead of being terrified out of his wits like any normal man, he found the sensation thrilling.

The man's excitement was of a sudden disgusting to Han and he let go of his shirt and then pulled back the hammer of his pistol with his thumb, squeezed the trigger to release the catch and eased the hammer back down gently. Then he tucked the gun back in his belt.

Now you might have thought that at this point Jed and Eli would combine together and kill Han on the spot; that wasn't how they worked though. That somebody, a mere boy at that, had stood up to one of them was such a novelty that they were quite enchanted. Jed turned to his brother with a broad smile on his face and said, 'Hey, Eli, you see that? Did you think that boy was going to kill me?'

'Sure looked like it from where I was sitting. I was sure you were for it that time. How come he didn't pull the trigger?'

'I don't rightly know. Hey, boy, how come you didn't pull that trigger?'

'I thought I'd let some other lucky bastard have the pleasure of killing you,' said Han, quite truthfully.

Jed roared with laughter, like this was the funniest thing he ever had heard. He bent over and slapped his thighs in obviously quite genuine amusement.

When he straightened up, he said to his brother, 'You hear that Eli? You hear what the boy said?'

Eli was grinning too. 'Yeah, I heard. See if he wants a drink.'

'You want a drink, boy?'

'Thanks, I've already had one glass of buttermilk. Any more than that and I'll be needing to get up to piss in the middle of the night.'

'You are something else again, boy, you know that? You looking for a job? I reckon we could use someone like you.'

'No, thank you. I already have enough work. I must be getting to bed now.'

'You look after yourself, you hear now?' said Jed, more jovial than he had been for days. 'What's your name, anyways?'

'My name is Jackson, Hohanonivah Jackson.' As Han gave the man his name, he watched him closely to see if it meant anything to him. Presumably he never even knew the full names of the two people whose lives had been

121

snuffed out by his boasting brother, because he merely nodded and went back to his table, hugely invigorated and cheered by the whole episode.

Outside, Han was trembling with a mixture of anger and relief. He had come very close to killing a man and probably being killed in turn by somebody else. This was the first time he had been involved in such an event, literally a matter of life and death so to speak. There are men like the Holts to whom the emotions aroused by such events are meat and drink, but for Han it had been a terrible experience. He felt sick and shaky, not so much from fear of having himself come close to death, but in the realization of how close he had come to killing a man.

It was while he was standing there in the darkness that the girl he had rescued earlier that day breezed up, saying, 'What you standing here like this for? You look like a hant. Has something scared you?'

Han turned to face her. 'It is nothing.

It will pass. What are you doing out and about? I thought you would have wanted a peaceful rest after seeing your relations murdered and having your house burned down.'

'You are not my father! What is it to you if I wish to go for an evening walk? I haven't been to town for some good long while. I aim to make the most of it.'

'I am going back to my room now to get a good night's sleep. I reckon that you could do worse than to do likewise.'

'You do, do you? Listen, what are we going to do tomorrow? How long are you planning that we should stay here?'

Han looked at her in surprise. 'There is no 'we' in the case. I rescued you from those Kiowa at some risk to myself, nearly getting knifed in the process. I have, moreover, stolen a horse for you and brought you here and paid for a room for you for the night. I have done all I need to do.'

Betty looked at him in amazement.

'That is the most I have heard you say at one go. You are not in general a one for talking, are you?'

'Come back to the boarding-house. The ponies are fine for tonight. In the morning, I have some business to see to and you can take the Indian's pony and go where you will. There is an end to the matter.'

Han strode off towards the boarding-house and was a little taken aback when the girl trailed after him. He had thought that she would not take heed of his words. Slowing down to allow her to catch up, he remarked, 'I am sorry to sound sharp. I have had a trying few days. My parents are both dead and I am not sure what road to take.'

Betty then astonished him by saying, 'Don't you think I'm at all pretty?'

'I have not set mind to the question. I think nothing about it, I have not noticed.'

She pulled a face. 'You are right charming and no mistake. What does it take for a girl to get you to take notice of her?'

'If Salome herself were to dance in front of me tonight, I don't think that I would set mind to her. I have a lot to think about.'

The two of them walked back in silence, Betty hugely affronted to be spoken to in that way. On Han's part, it was more that he was trying to fathom out in his mind the best way to proceed with matters touching upon the men who had killed his parents.

After he had seen Betty safely to her room, Han went to his own and lay on the bed without getting undressed. Then, fearing that he might dirty up the bedspread and confirm all the owner of the house thought about Indians, he took off his boots. Having done this, he lay down again and started going through things methodically.

Making a blood oath is easy and satisfying enough, especially when you are mad with grief. Still and all, it is a different kettle of fish than following through on the enterprise and really doing murder. Han had found out that night that he was not such a one, he was not able to shoot a man however just the cause.

It was unthinkable that those men should get away scot free though. He had observed that three of the others at that table also matched up to the descriptions which the men in the saloon had given him a couple of days previously. At least four of the five men were in town and had been drinking in that saloon tonight. Well, if he could not kill them himself, he would set the law on them. It was too late now to go rousing up the sheriff, but first thing in the morning he would see about having those men locked up and charged with murder.

Having fixed his plans for the following day, Han extinguished the candle and undressed. He had not had time to trouble about it when he was sleeping out, but every night that he had gone to bed for ten years, he had said the prayers that his parents had taught him. He supposed that the Lord was here in this town just as he was back home. He knelt by the bed and said, 'Lord, I am still minded to bring those skunks to justice. I am not the man to kill them myself though. We must see what happens tomorrow. Amen.'

★ ★ ★

Back at the saloon, the Holt brothers were in the mood for a party. One didn't often see women in that saloon, leastways not respectable ones. However, there were one or two prostitutes in the town who sold their favours to such of the Comancheros who wanted them. Also to some of the more upright citizens of the town as well, but this was done very much on the sly. Their dealings with the Comancheros were more open, usually took place in the bar-room and then moving on to one of the rented rooms on the floor above.

Word must have spread that the mood in the saloon was a little easier now, because, as the night progressed, more people drifted back in, including some of those who had scuttled out earlier when the Holts looked as though they were both in a murderous rage. Now, they were expansive and affable, treating those near to their table to free drinks and encouraging others to talk and make the evening lively. By around midnight, there was a festive air about the place.

One of the girls who dispensed her favours in exchange for hard cash was called Martha. She may have had the sort of name that you might associate with a Quaker or someone of that sort, but she was as willing and biddable a young woman as you could hope to encounter after a few drinks. Some nights, she went upstairs with several men, allowing them an hour each. She wasn't always in the bar-room, because she made private visits to men's homes as well as her more public appearances.

It was clear that Eli Holt had taken a bit of a shine to Martha just as soon as she had arrived that evening. He watched her carefully, trying to gauge if she was the sort of girl who would go along with his particular needs. These needs, into which we do not need to enquire overmuch, entailed ropes and such-like, combined with a little rough play. It was a rare whore who went twice with Eli, many of whom would show up next day sporting various cuts and bruises. Martha had, of course, heard all this, but reckoned that she was one who could tame a man given to that kind of thing.

So it was that at about one in the morning, Eli suggested to young Martha that they go upstairs and that she might, moreover, care to spend the night with him. Nothing loath, she agreed at once. Thinking herself a right shrewd bargainer, she insisted on payment in advance if she was going to be spending eight hours or so with just the one customer.

7

Next day, Han came down for breakfast at the boarding-house in a bright and cheery mood, like a man who has been grappling with a tricky problem and has decided at last upon the best course of action. The owner of the place noticed this.

'Why, Mr Jackson, you look like a man who is feeling braced with life this morning,' she said to him as he sat down at table.

'I am that, ma'am. And may I say that your bed was as soft and welcoming as that in my own home?'

The elderly woman simpered. Then she said, 'I do not know what time your companion will be rising today, I am sure. I would have thought she might be down before this.' She looked questioningly at him.

'I know nothing of her, I am afraid.

She was in a little difficulty on the road and I was able to be of some service to her. That is why I brought her to town.' He did not want to tell her of the kidnapping and murder by the two Kiowa. It would ignite her worst suspicions about Indians in general and next thing she would be watching him like a hawk, lest he attempt to burn down her own house and carry her off tied to his saddle.

'Well, I will say that you are a real gentleman, whatever the colour of your skin. Like a knight in armour.'

Han said, 'Tell me ma'am, where is the sheriff's office?'

'Why, it is just down the road a space. Walk down in the direction of the livery stable where you left your pony and you will see the office on the left-hand side. I hope there is nothing wrong?'

'No, nothing of the sort. It is just some small matter which requires my attention. It is nothing serious.'

At this point, Betty joined them,

looking sleepy and a little dishevelled. The woman eyed her disapprovingly. Han took the opportunity to rise, saying, 'If you will excuse me ladies, I must be off to the sheriff. I will be back later on.' He gave a courtly bow to the older woman, who blushed slightly.

Over at the saloon at about then, Jed Holt was banging on the door of the room which his brother was occupying, crying, 'Eli, it's gone nine of the clock, you lazy cow's son. Get up, we have to be moving.'

From inside the room, he heard Eli's muffled voice saying, 'I'm a-coming. Get down and wait for me, I'll be there directly.'

'Well, don't take all day, you idle bastard. We need to be in position in a couple of hours.'

Jed and the other five men were drinking coffee in the bar-room when Eli appeared. He looked terrible. He was white, shaky and had scratches across his face.

'God almighty, man,' said his brother,

132

'what happened to you? You look like shit!'

Eli growled something indistinctly and commenced to drink his coffee. Jed would not let the matter rest, saying, 'I mean it, man, what happened? Did that little spitfire do that to your face?'

'You gossip like a woman,' said Eli. 'I am not best minded to talk just now; we have business to undertake. Are you men all prepared?'

There were hurried grunts of assent. This looked like a day when it would be particularly unhealthy to get crosswise to Eli. When they were leaving, Jed took his brother to one side. 'Eli, what ails you? Tell me now.'

'There was some misunderstanding with that girl. It strikes me that we had best not return to town after today's game.'

'What the hell do you mean, 'misunderstanding'? What happened?'

Eli stared back at his brother. 'It does not signify. She is dead.'

'Dead? What are you talking of?'

'It is as I say, she died. It was unlucky. We had best not come back after this business with the Comancheros.'

'Ah, you stupid bastard. Not return today? Not ever you mean? What gets into you?'

'It can't be helped. Let's get going. I don't want to be here when that saloon keeper checks those rooms.'

There was nothing more to be said. It was not the first time that there had been such a 'misunderstanding'. Jed was just irritated that it should have happened in a town like this, which was such a useful bolthole. There it was, though, and there was nothing to be done about it.

When the seven of them were saddled up and riding down the road leading out of Tribulation, it would not have been possible to mistake the gang for anything other than a bunch of villains intent on robbery and murder. They had that reckless air about them of men who cared for little but their own needs.

As they trotted through town, Jed remarked to his brother, 'Look over yonder, there's that young Indian who was after nearly killing me last night. What business do you think he has with the sheriff?'

'I couldn't say,' said Eli, who was recovering his good humour by this time. 'Perhaps he is laying a complaint against you for breaching the peace.'

The two men guffawed with laughter and by the time they were a mile or so down the road, neither of them set much thought to what Eli had said earlier, touching upon the dead girl.

The sheriff was not in the dusty and, by the look of it, little used office. Han stood in there for a few minutes, waiting patiently before wandering back out into the street. A passer-by asked him, 'Looking for the sheriff? He'll be over there in the livery stable.'

Han thanked the man and then went off in search of the sheriff.

In Tribulation most of the ordinary

residents were fairly law-abiding and their misdemeanours and crimes did not, in the usual way of things, amount to much more than the odd case of wife-beating or public drunkenness. The rougher elements, who used the town as a kind of staging post for various illegal enterprises, took care that they harmed only their own kind. None of this involved the sheriff. He was being handsomely bribed to keep his eyes turned away from the gun-running, trade in stolen property and other, even less savoury activities. As long as they did not impinge upon the lives of Tribulation's regular citizens, Pete McGuire was only too happy to see and hear nothing. He was over at the livery stable that morning to see about buying a horse, but that is by the by.

First Pete knew about it was when a good-looking young Indian dressed in white man's clothes came up to him and asked diffidently, 'Excuse me sir, are you the sheriff?'

'That I am,' he replied. 'How can I help you?'

'I want to report a murder. Well, two murders actually.'

Pete McGuire stared hard at the young man, who was in truth little more than a boy. 'Is this a joke, son? Because if so, you'll find that there are serious penalties for wasting the time of a peace officer.'

'It's no joke, sir. My parents were murdered a few days ago and I believe that the men who did it are now in this town. I want to see them arrested.'

Abandoning his plans for the buying of a new horse, McGuire sighed and said to Han, 'Well, I guess you better come over to the office. This better not turn out to be a mare's nest though, I'm telling you now.'

No man likes to be buffaloed into acting against his own best interests and McGuire was no exception. It sat ill with him to have this young Indian come in and start creating trouble. He had already had enough to contend with over the last day or two, what with Den Sothill's widow wailing and complaining in his office that her husband had been killed. He had no great love for the Holt brothers, but at the same time not the least desire to go up against them. All he wanted was for them to conclude whatever business they had in his town and then up sticks and leave; the sooner the better.

The shooting of Den Sothill had put Pete McGuire into a bad mood because it went against the grain of his principle that the only violence in town should be inflicted by the bad boys against each other. He surely did not like to see an ordinary citizen gunned down in this way.

When they got to the sheriff's office, he invited Han to be seated and tell his tale. Han did so, right up to the incident in the saloon when he had heard his parents' names being bandied around.

McGuire said, 'You know the name of any of these men?'

'No, sir.'

'You got any firm evidence to link them to this crime you tell me about?'

'No.'

'Can you even swear that those men you saw in the saloon last night were the same ones you have been tracking?'

Han shook his head reluctantly. 'No, I can't swear to it. I am sure in my own mind though.'

Pete McGuire lit his pipe. 'It is awful thin, son. I don't say that you are wrong about it, mind. There are some very strange and undesirable types coming to this town. Howsoever, I cannot see how you expect me to make out a warrant on what you have told me so far. Both Esther and Patrick are common enough names. You have no reason to think that they were talking about your ma and pa.'

The two of them sat there for a minute or two, each sunk in his own thoughts. From the description that the Indian had given him, McGuire was certain-sure that the Holts were the people involved. He could easily believe that they would kill an elderly couple for a pot of gold coins. Since the alleged crime had taken place far from his town though, he was not overly eager to start investigating it. The Holts of all people! He had been horrified when they fetched up in the town after an absence of almost a year. Trouble followed those boys like shit round a shirt-tail. With luck, they would light out soon and he would not have to deal with them face to face, a prospect which filled him with dread. He had strong suspicions that there were probably a dozen warrants floating around for the Holts. He did not know for sure, of course, and neither did he want to. He just wished that they would take themselves off out of his town.

Han was thinking that this man had no intention of helping him in any respect. If he wanted those men to face a court, he was going to have to arrest them himself and take them there. He half wished that he could have ignored his raising and just blown that fellow's head off the night before.

While the two of them were musing along these lines, the street door burst open and a man said in an agitated voice, 'Sheriff, you got to come over to the hotel right away. There been murder done there!'

'The hell there has,' said McGuire, getting to his feet. To Han, he said, 'I'm sorry for your loss, boy, but I don't see what I can do.'

'You mean you will do nothing and hope that those killers leave town quickly so that they are somebody else's problem.'

This was so sharp and truthful that the sheriff said nothing in response, bar, 'Get out of here. I got more pressing concerns than your story.'

* * *

The Holts and their gang had chosen the perfect spot for their ambush. The road towards Midway passed through a

141

kind of gully, with slopes going up on either side. Trees were growing on the slopes and there were boulders and rocks large enough to conceal men. All that was needed was to lie in wait for their prey and then start blasting at them and their horses as soon as they came into sight. Three of them took places on one side of the road and four on the other.

Jed was worried about his brother. Both Eli and Jed had a very strange view of death, which was not a thing either of them feared in the least, but there was about Eli this morning an air that Jed did not much care for. Whatever had happened last night with the girl had affected him badly, which was not at all like the man. Jed was hoping that Eli would play his part that day without behaving in too foolhardy a fashion. While it was true that as long as they all stayed behind cover, shooting away at the Comancheros, there was every chance that this affair would pass off to their satisfaction, it was also the

142

fact that they were probably going to be outnumbered by their opponents. This made it essential that every one of them kept his head and just stayed down.

The sides of the gully flattened out at the top of the rise, which was where they had tethered their horses. Eli had taken up his position there, sheltered by a clump of trees. Jed went over to him. 'Eli, are you feeling all right? Tell me now, is there anything troubling you?'

Eli gave him a ghastly smile. 'Troubling me, boy? No, no, I tell you I never felt better in my life. Nothing can touch me this day. Not the law, not bullets, not even the dead spirits of those we killed.'

Jed looked at him in horror. 'Dead spirits? Eli, what the hell are you talking about? What dead spirits? I have never heard you say anything of this sort in the whole course of your life. What ails you?'

'I told you, there is nothing wrong.'

'Do you want that we should call this business off? We can ride down to Texas and find another thing to do.'

Eli smiled that weird smile again. 'No Jed, I tell you now that the dead are on our side. We need not be afeared of anybody, living or dead.'

His brother just stared at him, lost for words. Then a man on the opposite ridge called out, 'I can see them coming. They are two miles or so off from us.' Jed skittered down the slope to take up his own position behind a boulder.

* * *

Pete McGuire nearly fainted on the spot when he saw what was waiting for him in the room above the saloon. He had seen some grim sights in his day, but nothing to match this. There is no need to go into detail about what had befallen young Martha. It is enough to say that she was roped to the bed and looked as though she had died hard.

'Jesus Christ,' gasped the sheriff, 'I

never saw the like. Who was in this room?'

'Eli Holt,' said the owner of the saloon. 'Sheriff, Martha was, as you might say, a little loose, but she didn't deserve nothing like this.'

'Nobody deserves a death like this,' said McGuire. 'Where is Eli and his brother now?'

'I couldn't say. They rode out this morning at a little after nine. They told me that they would be back this evening.'

Pete McGuire gave one final look at the wreckage lashed to the bed and then closed the door, saying, 'I want this room kept locked, you hear me?'

In that mysterious way that happens in small towns, word had gotten round about the unfortunate Martha's death. Now she may only have been a saloon girl and prostitute, but Martha was a good-hearted soul and had been popular in the town. More to the point, she was one of them. She lived there and was a resident of Tribulation, which put her untimely passing in an altogether different category from that of some comanchero who might happen to get himself knifed in a darkened allyway. There had been mutterings about the shooting of Den Sothill and now another person had died.

When Pete McGuire walked out of the saloon, he found a little cluster of concerned citizenry milling about on the sidewalk. One of them was the blacksmith, who asked outright, 'Sheriff, what are you fixing to do about this?' There were murmurs of, 'Yeah Pete, what you going to do?' and similar.

'This here is a matter for me, not for you men,' began Pete, but he was drowned out by angry voices which were raised in protest. He waited for the noise to subside before he spoke again. 'Listen, I liked Martha as much as any of you. I cannot act alone though. If you men are keen to see the killer brought to justice, then you will have to help me. I am not giving away too much of my enquiry if I let you know that she was in the room occupied by one of the Holt brothers. If any man wishes now to be sworn in as deputy, just for the duration, then we will get up a regular posse and go in search of them.'

The angry cries that something had to be done died away to nothing once the case was presented to them in this wise. To be fair to those men, they earnestly wanted something done about the murder and hoped to see Martha's killer hang for the crime. At the same time, they all had livelihoods to tend and not one of them felt inclined to step forward to volunteer for a posse. The Holts were a mite too well known for that.

'Yes,' said McGuire, 'and that is just about what I expected. You come clamouring here for me to do something, but none of you is exactly keen to lend a hand. I will do what I am able and that is all that I am saying.' He turned to go, when a voice called out from the back of the crowd.

'I will volunteer. Swear me in as a deputy and I will ride with you this minute to hunt down the man who did this.'

Everybody turned and stared in amazement at the young man who had spoken. They saw a tall, well-built Indian wearing regular clothes. The sheriff snorted. 'Are you men going to let this boy be the only one who will help me? Is that how much you care about Martha?'

There was an embarrassed silence. At length, McGuire said, 'All right, son, you follow me now.' He walked back to his office, with Han walking alongside him. When they were inside, McGuire invited the boy to take a seat. 'When you were telling me about seeing one of the men you was searching for in the saloon last night, you left out part of the story, leastways judging by what the fellow who owns that place told me. By which I mean, that part touching upon your sticking a gun to his throat and coming close to shooting him. How come you did not tell me that?'

'I did not see that it had any bearing on the matter.'

'You are a likely enough young man, but do not go getting too smart for your own good.'

'I will remember your words. I suppose that the men I saw last night were the Holt brothers, one of them having killed that girl?'

'That is so.'

'Well then, what are we going to do?'

'I am thinking.'

'That will not catch them. While you sit here thinking, they might be getting clean away from here.'

'That was one of the things I was thinking,' said McGuire grimly. 'I was thinking that would be no bad thing and might save us all a mort of trouble.'

'Are you going to look for them?'

'All in good time. If you will help me, it must be done legal and above board. You are over twenty-one?'

'I do not believe so. From what I

know, I lack some two years or more until I am that age.'

'No, you damned fool. You must be twenty-one for me to swear you in. I will ask you again, are you twenty-one?'

'Yes, I am.'

The sheriff poked around in a drawer of his desk and came out with a dull-looking piece of tin and a sheet of printed words. 'Repeat the oath after me,' he said.

Han did so and was handed the little star.

'You are now a duly authorized deputy, leastways until we catch up with those boys. You know you are likely to come to a bloody end on this enterprise?'

'I have thought on this. If it brings those who killed my parents to justice, then that is fine by me.'

'Well, you're a damned fool. Go and fetch your horse. I suppose you *have* a horse?'

'Yes, I shall fetch her from the livery stable. Shall I meet you back here?'

'No, I'll walk along with you. You have a pistol, I see. Do you have a rifle too?'

Han told him that he did and the two of them went across the street to get their horses.

8

Here is how things were set up for the robbery that the Holts had instigated. Rick, John and one of the men that Eli and Jed had recruited were concealed on one side of the road and the Holts and the other two men were on the other. It had been agreed that Eli was to give the signal for the attack to begin by firing his rifle at the approaching group. Eli would have it so because he said that he could not trust anybody else to gauge the precise and right moment to fire. Jed was still uneasy in his mind about his brother, but short of knocking the man down and trussing him up, he did not see what was to be done.

They heard the horses before they saw them. As soon as they came into sight around a little bend and started down the straight section of road where the Holt brothers and their gang were hiding, Jed's misgivings were redoubled. There were twelve of them. Lord knows what they had in the wagon, but they were riding like a military formation, with outriders ahead of the main body. If the road had not been passing through this narrow space, Jed thought that they would probably have been putting out flankers as well. He knew then that the smart move was to remain silent and let these men pass by unmolested. The whole stunt that he and his brother had mounted was centred around taking the men by surprise. These men looked like they were just waiting for trouble. There would be no question of taking them unawares. He turned round to signal to Eli and nearly choked in amazement.

Eli was mounting his horse and staring ahead of him in a demented fashion, like he could see things that nobody else could. Jed didn't know whether this was a result of Eli overindulging in whiskey for the last few days, or if his brother had just gone loco. Not that it mattered much now, because Eli was in the saddle and moving his horse forward, plainly about to ride down the slope to his almost certain death. 'Eli,' cried Jed, 'what are you doing?'

Either his brother couldn't hear him or didn't care, because he spurred on his horse, speeding up into a canter as he went down the slope towards the riders below. People said that he and his brother knew instinctively what the other was going to do. This time though, Jed was as taken aback by his brother's antics as everybody else. He ran up to where his own horse was standing and mounted up himself.

Meantime, Eli Holt was careering down the side of that gully towards the road. He gave what sounded like a rebel yell, shouting 'Yeee hah!' at the top of his voice. The he pulled out one pistol and fired it into the air. The men posted on the other side of the ride started shooting at the horses, but had to stop after a few rounds, for fear of hitting Eli, who was now on the roadway and galloping full pelt towards the riders. Jed was following him down, also as fast as he could get his horse to move on that uncertain terrain.

It had taken a second or two for the Comancheros to react, for all that they looked as though they might have been expecting trouble. Some of them were firing towards the men up on the slope, while others turned their attention to the Holts. By the time they knew what was happening though, Eli and Jed had ridden past them and once they were clear, the other members of the ambush could start up a withering fire against the men in the road.

Eli rode his horse back up towards the ridge, with Jed following on. They dismounted, pulled out their rifles and began shooting down at the men clustered around the wagon. And then, just as though it was looking like the Holt brothers were going to pull off one more of their mad stunts successfully, another group of Comancheros rode up from the opposite direction. At this point, both Eli and Jed could see that the case was hopeless and so, without another thought, they ran back to their horses, jumped up and cantered off in the general direction of Tribulation.

'You mad fool,' said Jed. 'What for did you go galloping down there?'

'You remember that boy we killed, back end of seventy-two; the one where we set fire to his cabin and shot him when he came out?'

'Sure I remember him. What about him?'

'He was there, Jed,' said Eli, his eyes glittering and his face feverish. 'I seed him there, standing by a tree, down nigh to those Comancheros. He was coming for me, Jed, that's why I rode on past him.'

Jed looked closely at his brother and then said urgently, 'You been hit, man, you got blood on your back. Hold up, stop your horse now and let me take a look.'

They halted and Eli allowed him to untuck his shirt and look underneath. The bullet had entered at the front, somewhere near Eli's liver and travelled all the way through, coming out of his back near his kidneys.

'How bad is it?' asked Eli.

'It's nothing man, nothing at all. We had best move on a space, just in case anybody is following us. Then we must stop and I shall dress your wound.'

Eli had a moment of lucidity. 'Nothing, you say? You are a lousy liar, Jed. I am shot to pieces. I don't think that I shall live much longer.' As Jed looked closer, he could see that Eli's pants were soaked in blood. He was bleeding like a stuck hog.

Jed dismounted and tried to help his brother down from his horse. Eli collapsed in his arms and he lowered him gently to the ground. When Han and the sheriff rode up a half-hour later, that's how they found the pair of them, with Jed cradling his dead brother in his arms.

'What happened to your brother?' asked Pete McGuire, his hand gripping his pistol, although not pulling it from the holster.

'He's dead. He was shot.'

'Who shot him? Was it you?'

'Why would I shoot my own brother?'

'I don't know, you mad bastard. There is no accounting for what the two of you do. There is a suspicion that your brother killed a girl last night. I don't know what part you might have had in the business, but I must take you back to town under arrest.'

Jed Holt was staring at Han. 'What is that Indian doing here? He was all for killing me last night.'

The sheriff shrugged. 'I am not sure that I blame him for that. He says you and your brother killed his parents.'

Jed looked genuinely puzzled and confused. 'His parents? I haven't killed an Indian for a good while. He is mixing me up with somebody else. I think that you should arrest him for trying to kill me.'

'Don't you set mind to him. You are in trouble enough yourself,' said Pete McGuire.

Han said softly, 'My parents were not Indians. They were an old couple north of here, up near Sand Creek. Esther and Patrick Jackson. You seemed to remember them well enough the other night when your brother was bragging about robbing them.'

Jed looked at the young man with new interest. 'Well now, you don't say so. That goes some distance towards explaining why you nearly shot me last night. Why didn't you? Yellow?'

The sheriff interrupted at this point, saying, 'You have not yet told me how your brother died.'

'We were ambushed by some Comancheros. All my friends were killed and only we survived. It was a tragedy.'

'Folk in town is all riled up about

159

that girl,' said McGuire. 'I don't think that they would look kindly on me if I did not bring somebody back. Your brother is dead, which means that you might have to answer for it.'

'I didn't kill her. It is not my style.'

'Maybe not, but there are those who are still sore about you shooting Den Sothill. We will see what happens.'

Asking Han to cover him, which that young man did with the greatest pleasure, the sheriff took Holt's pistol and handcuffed his hands in front of him. He then desired him to mount his horse. All the time, Jed and Han were watching each other, both wondering if the young man's grief and anger would overcome him to the extent that he would shoot unexpectedly. This same thought was going through the mind of the sheriff, because it would have solved the whole question in a very neat and tidy fashion. Had he taken Jed Holt alone, it is possible that he might just have let him go on his way, because he was damned if he knew how he was going to get the man to a trial.

McGuire and Han managed to hoist the dead man over the saddle of his horse and secure him there. While they were doing so, his brother said angrily, 'Hey, mind what you're about with him. He is a man, you know, not a side of bacon.' The sheriff straightened up and stared contemptuously at Jed.

'You think he was a man? You should see what he did to that poor girl he misused. You think that a real man would have served a girl so? I am telling you, your brother was a beast. You are of the same breed.'

As the three living men and the dead one rode back to Tribulation, Jed Holt said to Han, 'You still ain't told me why you didn't pull the trigger last night. God knows you had cause enough.'

'I did not wish to be like you, I guess. It is a hell of a thing to shoot a fellow being. I did not want the weight of it on my conscience.'

Holt laughed shortly. 'It is just as I thought, you're yellow.'

They lodged Holt in the poky little lockup at the back of McGuire's office. The space was no bigger than a broom closet and really only meant to hold drunks overnight and that kind of thing. Which left the sheriff with the problem of what to do with him in the long term. He had taken quite a liking to Han, who was an amiable and respectful young man, and talked the matter over with him while they walked around the town.

'The problem is,' he told Han, 'I cannot just go gallivanting off to deliver Holt to anybody else. I'll warrant that he is wanted in a half-dozen different places and if he was took to somewhere with a telegraph office and railroad, then they would love to have him. I think he would hang, if not for your parents then for other equally bad crimes.'

'Where is the nearest such place that he could be taken?' asked Han.

'Hopetown would fit the bill. It is forty miles from here and I know the sheriff.'

Han said nothing for a time and then remarked, 'I could take him there. I am still a deputy, am I not?'

'You?' said McGuire. 'You are little more than a boy. He would escape and probably murder you into the bargain. I would not wish to take responsibility for it.'

'What will you do then? Provide him with free board and lodging 'til he dies of old age?'

'You know,' McGuire said, 'for a youngster, you have a right sharp way with you. Do you really want to take him to Hopetown?'

'I don't want to, but otherwise he might walk free. You are holding him now, but he has not really broke any laws that you can put on him. If as you say there are warrants for him elsewhere, then getting him to another town is the only answer.'

'I am not sure how good a scheme it would be to let you take that man off across forty miles of deserted country. One of you might kill the other.'

'Well, it's nothing to you whether we both live or die, at least it will all be somebody else's responsibility.'

'Yes, I have thought of that too. It would mean sleeping overnight somewhere.'

Pete McGuire was still dubious about the whole thing and asked Han to call by his office later that day. They had no sooner parted, than Betty popped up and desired to know what had been going on and where Han had been.

'I call it mean of you to go off like that without telling me. You are having all the fun and I have been stuck with that sour-faced old witch.'

'It was not much fun seeing that dead girl, nor lifting a dead man on to a horse, neither. Your idea of fun is a strange one.'

'There is nothing doing in this town,' said Betty. 'I would like to go somewhere more exciting. What say that you and me move out in the next few days?'

'I have told you one time already.

There is no 'we' or 'us' in the case. I am not answerable for you and there is an end of it. You must make your own way now.'

Betty made a face. 'Is it true that they are going to lynch that man in the sheriff's office?'

'Where did you hear such a thing?' asked Han, startled. 'Who said that they want to lynch him?'

'I did not collect his name. I heard some men talking.'

Han said no more to the girl, but went straight in search of the sheriff. When he tracked him down, he asked bluntly, 'Is it true that there is talk of lynching Holt?'

'I shouldn't wonder. People are right riled up about Martha.'

'But I thought his brother did that?'

'His brother's dead. Folk want somebody to blame. Some of them are still angry about Den Sothill and you can't lay that at anybody's door but Jed Holt.'

'What will you do?'

Pete McGuire sighed. 'If you will really engage to take him away from town tomorrow, then I reckon I will spend the night in my office to make sure that nobody gets excited and tries to storm the place. There has never been a lynching in this town and I don't aim to see one being done now.'

'Wouldn't that solve your problem just as neatly?'

'Listen, young fellow, I may not be much of a sheriff, but there are some things I will not have: hanging a man without trial is one of them.'

Back at the boarding-house, the old woman was vastly impressed to see that Han was wearing a star. 'My, my,' she said. 'I will tell you the truth, I thought that you were some shiftless wanderer when you arrived here. Yet here you are now as a deputy. What will happen next?'

'What will chiefly happen next, ma'am, is that I am travelling to Hopetown first thing tomorrow morning. I was wondering if you could put together enough food to last two men for two days. The sheriff will pay for it.'

'Two men? What, you are going on a journey with Pete McGuire?'

'Not exactly, no. I am escorting the man he has locked up to Hopetown, so that the sheriff there may deal with him.'

'Well, you don't say so. Just you and that man whose brother killed that poor girl? Lord, I hope that he does not cut your throat on the journey or something of that nature.'

'Yes, ma'am, I have much the same hope myself.'

At which point Betty entered the room and said, 'What journey? You said nothing to me of a journey when we spoke earlier. Where are you going?'

'He is going to Hopetown,' said the owner of the boarding-house, before Han could answer.

'Hopetown?' exclaimed Betty. 'Say, I've always wanted to visit there. We can travel together and make a holiday of it.'

Han decided that the time had come for plain speaking. 'Listen, I do not want to appear rude, but one or two things must be made plain. I am not connected with you in any wise and we are not going to travel anywhere together. Next is where I will be escorting a bad man to that town and will need to keep my eye upon him. You and me will part company for good and all tomorrow and go our separate ways. After I have seen this man safe in Hopetown, I intend to return to my own home. This is all that I will say on this subject.'

Having said his piece, Han then went upstairs to get his things together. A little while later, there was a knock on the door. When he opened it, Betty was standing there. She had tears in her eyes and looked to be genuinely upset. 'Can I come in?' she asked.

'Land sakes,' said Han, horrified at such impropriety. 'You cannot come into my bedroom with just the two of us alone. Wait downstairs and we will go for a walk. There is nothing to say though. I am not changing my mind.'

Ten minutes later, Hohanonivah Jackson and the young girl were strolling along the street, causing it must be said, a few raised eyebrows. It was not as provoking perhaps as the sight of other mixed pairings would have been, but seeing an Indian walking side by side in what seemed an intimate manner with a white girl did not sit easy with many of those who saw it.

'I do not know why you will not take me with you,' said Betty. 'I have no folks and nowhere to go. It is right mean of you.'

'I have already said that this is not going to happen. I want to go home.'

'Take me with you.'

Han stopped dead in his tracks. 'Have you lost your mind? I can't have a young girl living with me. It would compromise us both.'

'I don't see that at all. Who lives at your place?'

'Nobody, right now. That is another

reason why I wish to get back. The Lord knows what mischief is being wrought there by thieves or suchlike.'

'Well,' said the girl, suddenly meek, 'if you would have it so, then I guess that there is no more to be said on the subject. What time will you leave tomorrow morning?'

The sudden change in tone made Han suspicious. 'Why do you ask me that?'

'Lordy, I just wanted to say goodbye. You saved my life, I would not have you think that I was not mindful of that.'

'I hope to be on the road a little after dawn.'

'That's mighty early. Perhaps we had best say our farewells this evening instead.'

After parting in this fairly amicable way from the girl, Han headed over to the sheriff's office. He was relieved to note that there did not appear to be a lynch mob gathering outside and that Pete McGuire was sitting at his desk, relaxed as could be, talking to a friend.

When he saw Han, he said, 'Ah, just in time, son. Holt wants you to favour him with a little conversation. You don't need to, but I suppose that you will be spending long enough in his company over the next two days, so you might as well.'

'All right,' said Han, 'I will speak to him now.'

He was shown into the back room, half of which was separated into a barred compartment like a cage at a zoo. Jed Holt grinned at him. 'Well boy, I did not think that it would come to this and that's a fact. I comprehend that you are to escort me north in the morning to Hopetown. You know what this means?'

'I suppose,' said Han, 'that it means that you are likely to hang. That is, if the sheriff there knows of any murders you are wanted for.'

The other man gave a short laugh. 'There may be one or two such. Tell me now, why you did not kill me last night?'

171

Han shrugged. 'I told you. When it came to it, I could not do it. What more will you know?'

'I wish you had. My brother is dead and I think that I will not be attending his funeral.'

'What happened to those men you rode out with this morning?'

'Dead, most likely. Why?'

'Were any of them there when you killed my ma and pa?'

'Yeah, two of them were there. I reckon that they are both deceased by now, which must be a satisfaction to you.'

'There were five there at my parents' place. What happened to the other one?'

'I shot him myself. There is only me to answer for it all now.'

'Why did you want to see me?' asked Han.

'I will tell you. I do not wish to hang like a dog. It is a dreadful business. Did you ever see a hanging?'

Han shook his head.

'Most times, the neck is not broke and the fellow chokes to death, kicking his life out on the end of the rope. Usually he makes water and fouls himself too. What I would ask of you is that if I am to die, you shoot me on the journey and then say that it was while I was trying to escape. It is nothing to you and you will be revenged just the same. What do you say?'

Han stood up. 'I will think on it. I shall see you in the morning.'

As he left, McGuire followed him out into the street and said, 'Are you up to this game tomorrow? I have took a liking to you and it would sadden me to think of anything happening to you. He is a tricksy and dangerous one, you know.'

'It will be fine. Will you give me a letter for the sheriff in Hopetown?'

'Yes, I will. I am going to sit up here all night, so the sooner after dawn you get here, the sooner I can get to sleep.'

'It will not be long after sun-up. I will bid you good night now.'

As he walked off, the sheriff stared after him in perplexity. I wonder, he thought to himself, if that young fellow is planning to finish off Holt when the two of them are in the middle of nowhere. Not that he taxed his brain overlong on the question. It was enough for him that the man in the back of the office would be out of his way in a few hours.

The woman at the boarding-house had prepared food for the journey. Since she would be billing the town for it, Han guessed that she would not be doing too badly out of the deal. He retired early, having said his farewells to both the old woman and Betty. He did not look to see either of them again as he would be starting out very early the next day.

As he lay in bed, Han thought about what Jed Holt had asked him. Perhaps in that position, he might feel the same way himself. Pretty much anything would, he thought, be preferable to a public hanging with all the indignities which such a death entailed. He owed the man nothing though and did not trust him. In the end, he decided that he could think the question over on the journey and had no occasion to fret about it that night.

9

Han woke as the sun rose above the horizon. Growing up on a farm, this was how his body's cycle had always worked: rise at dawn and go to bed soon after dusk. He dressed, collected everything together and slipped quietly from the house. There was nobody about as he walked to the sheriff's office. Pete McGuire was still seated at his desk and he looked pleased to see Han. 'Well, you are an early riser and no mistake,' he said cheerfully.

They went into the back to find that Jed Holt was also awake. McGuire had cuffed his hands in front of him before he went to sleep the night before, which made him a little safer than he would otherwise have been. He greeted Han, saying, 'Sure is a fine day for a little ride out.'

McGuire said, 'Just keep your mouth

shut, Holt. I have had to lose a night's sleep protecting your worthless neck. Late last night, I received word of some gunfight not far from here. I will take oath that that is how your brother died.'

'Talking of which,' said Holt, 'I hope that you will see my brother receives a decent funeral, such as befits his status?'

'He will be buried as a pauper in an unmarked grave nigh to the church, if that is what you mean,' replied the sheriff, who was feeling tetchy from having to sit up the whole entire night in this way.

Holt leaned close to the sheriff and said, 'I catch ahold of you without these cuffs on, you are dead. You know this?'

McGuire gave him a shove, which almost sent him over. 'Do not provoke me by this vain bluster today, Jed. I am not in the right mood for such foolishness.' Turning to Han, he said, 'I will walk over to the livery stable with you and see you both mounted and safely on your way. Take my advice and do not take those cuffs off him for any purpose. He can get his drawers down if he needs to answer any calls of nature and I doubt that it will matter if he cannot get undressed if you are sleeping out tonight.'

Once they had the horses dealt with and before they had mounted, the sheriff offered Han the key to the handcuffs. Han said, 'You know what, it would make more sense if I was not carrying that thing. It would be open invitation for Holt to try and murder me in the night so that he could free himself. Surely they can saw the things off when we get to Hopetown?'

Holt gave a roar of laughter when he heard this. 'If that boy is not the sharpest one of all of us. He puts you to shame in the brains department, McGuire.'

So it was that Hohanonivah Jackson set off north, riding side by side with the man who had murdered his parents. He kept a little behind the man he was escorting, because he would not have put it past Holt to try and jump him, chained together though his hands were. Holt whistled a jaunty little tune as though they were going hunting together, rather than setting off on an expedition which was likely to end in his ignominious death.

Holt made no attempt to talk to Han. As for Han, he had his pistol tucked loosely in his belt, ready to use it at a moment's notice. His rifle was also loaded and it was only now after they had set out, that he began to wonder how it would work out at night. If he fell asleep, this man would make sure to steal his weapons and kill him into the bargain. It was while he was considering deep about this problem that he caught sight of a rider ahead. The person did not want to be seen and the very first thought in Han's mind was that this a plot to free Holt.

He said to the man, 'Hold up now. Rein in your horse.'

Holt did so and said, 'What's to do?'

'Look up ahead. There is a rider

behind those trees. He is waiting for us. Would this be perhaps some friend of yours?'

'I do not think that I have any friends remaining alive. Your guess is as good as mine as to who it is and what is his purpose.'

'We shall soon see,' said Han grimly. He pulled out the rifle and cocked it. 'Now you ride on ahead of me and I tell you now that if there is any shooting, you at least will be the first to die with a bullet in your back.'

They moved forward slowly and then of a sudden, the rider trotted forth, at which point Han halted and raised the rifle to his shoulder.

'Hidy,' said Betty. 'I figured that you would not really mind me coming along. I will be no trouble and have brought a picnic of my own.'

Han was stumped for words adequate to the situation. All those he first came up with were curse-words and he was too much of a gentleman to utter them in the presence of a lady. While he was struggling to express his feelings, Jed Holt chimed in, saying, 'Why hello, young lady. It will be nice to have some female company on this trip. This young fellow is pleasant enough, but he does not talk much. You will act on me like a regular tonic.'

'Shut up, Holt,' said Han roughly. 'Betty, it is not to be thought of. You must go back to town.'

'Not a bit of it, Betty,' said Holt. 'You will brighten up our day considerable.'

Han rode up behind the other man and jabbed him in the back with his rifle. 'I said keep quiet. Betty, you must go back. This man would kill the two of us as soon as look at us. I am taking him to Hopetown only to see if they have some case against him. Then I am going home.'

Betty's pretty but weak face took on an expression of mulish obstinacy. 'You can't *make* me go back. I will just ride along with you. You won't even know I am here.'

Holt was chuckling to himself. 'This

is surely the strangest journey of this sort which I could have imagined. Being sent to my death in the company of two young people who are no more than children. It is not how I ever saw my career as ending.'

'Never mind your career,' said Han, 'it is your life which will end shortly if you do not remain silent. Betty, please go back.'

'I will not,' she said.

'All right, Holt. Trot on.'

The three of them set off like this. In the lead was Jed Holt and following him at a little distance was Han. Behind the two of them rode Betty. There was nothing that Han could really do to prevent the girl from following them, but he figured that if he just ignored her, she might lose interest and go away. She was not of that stamp though, being quite indifferent to being snubbed in this wise. After they had been riding along the track for a while, she began to chatter in her usual, inconsequential way.

'It is a lovely day. Han, you have not yet told me your friend's name.'

'He is not my friend. This man killed my parents.'

'Well, he must still have a name. What is it?'

Holt called back to her, 'I am Jed Holt and I am honoured to make your acquaintance.'

'My, ain't you got fancy manners! Han, can I ride next to Mr Holt? I would like to chat a little to him.'

'Are you out of your mind? He is a killer. One mistake and he will get free and kill us both.'

'Surely that cannot be true. Mr Holt, would you really kill us if you got the chance?'

'Me, kill a charming young girl like you? I tell you straight, I am what you might term a misunderstood man. Your friend there, he says many hard things of me, but half of them are not true. I never yet killed anybody except in self-defence.'

It was plain as a pikestaff to Han that

Holt was sweetening up the foolish girl for some purpose. Most likely, he hoped to sow dissension between him and Betty and then somehow exploit this to make a move towards escaping. Short of gagging the man, there was little that he could do to stop it. Holt knew as well as he did himself that all his threats to shoot a helpless man who had his hands fastened together were meaningless.

Holt said to him, 'Listen, Han or whatever your name is, how come you were raised by those old people?'

'It does not signify,' said Han. 'It is nothing to the purpose to talk of it.'

'Come on, boy, there must be a fine story there. It will pass the time.'

'Do you think that I will tell you the story of my first family's murder just to entertain you for a while? You are mistaken.'

'Was it the Sand Creek Massacre?' enquired Holt shrewdly. 'That is only just down the way from that old couple's place. Going by that headband of yours, I would say that you are Cheyenne. Am I right?'

'You talk more than the girl. I have no wish to say anything of this.'

'It is as I thought,' said Holt, 'your real parents were killed at Sand Creek. I knew it.'

Han knew that Jed Holt was trying to goad him, but he could not hear his parents talked of in this way by this man. He said to Holt, 'You keep my parents out of your goddamned mouth, you hear what I tell you now? Otherwise, I will take you up on the suggestion you made to me last night.'

Holt gave a short, barking laugh. 'Well boy, I reckon that offer's off the table. After all, you got a witness now. You think that girl could be got to keep quiet about it if you shot me now? I do not think so.'

They rode along in silence for a while, even Betty not wishing to speak. Truth to tell, she was beginning to wonder if this had been the best idea that she had ever had. She was not a perfect fool and it was becoming obvious to her that there was going to be some species of friction between Han and his prisoner.

'Han,' she said in a quiet voice, 'do you think I should turn back?'

'Do what you will,' he said, 'I have no more use for you than I do for him,' indicating Holt.

The three of them kept going for another hour or so, with none of them speaking. Then Holt said, 'When you grabbed ahold of me in the saloon the other night, I thought you was a man. It is some good long while since any man has dared to lay hands on me. But all your talk about not wishing to shoot me and so on is just a way of saying that you are yellow. You did not pull the trigger because you were afeared to do it.'

Han did not reply. He could feel rage bubbling up within him and was hoping to hold it back. Being like this in the close proximity to the man who had helped kill his ma and pa was proving a sorer trial than he would have thought. It was perhaps not altogether a bad thing that Betty had come along. If it was not for her being there, he might well get into a killing rage.

'Betty,' he said, 'I am sorry for being rough to you. There was no call for me to do so. I hope I have not upset you?'

The girl smiled at him gratefully. He was ashamed to see that she had been crying and he had not even noticed. She was perhaps not quite as tough as she made out. 'I'm sorry about your family,' she said. 'It must be right hard to lose not one set of parents, but two. I know, because like I told you, I lost my own family when I was little.'

'It is a hard row to hoe,' said Han.

They stopped after noon to eat and drink. Han insisted that Holt sat a distance from him and Betty, saying that being close to Holt took away his appetite and made him feel nauseous. After a short rest, they set off again. Holt was not that talkative himself now and just plodded along a little ahead of the other two. Han and Betty chatted in a desultory way. Once the girl dropped her act and behaved as her real self, Han found her tolerably good company. He was not sorry now that she had forced her way into the business and thought that it would have been grim enough if it had just been him and Holt by their own selves.

The little party continued with only a few brief stops until it was getting on for dusk. They were close to a little wood and Han said that they would tie up the horses there and make camp for the night. He kept a watch on Jed Holt and asked Betty to gather up some wood for a fire. Again, he made Holt sit away from them.

There could not be the least question of him and Betty both sleeping. The murderous rogue would be on them in the night and it would likely prove the death of them. Han said, 'I do not aim to sleep tonight. Betty, you sleep over there aways behind me and you, Holt, just lie where you are. I shall sit here with the rifle and before God, if you move a foot from that place, I shall shoot you.'

'I don't think that you will be able to remain awake all night,' said Holt.

'I tell you straight, I do not care what you think on it. Just be sure that I will have this rifle pointing in your direction until dawn. If you wish to try your luck, then see what results. Do not blame me for the consequence though, it will be upon your own head.'

Betty did not show any inclination to sleep and instead sat and talked to Han. She told him of her life on the farm, which, for all her complaining and talk of being made to work like a slave, did not sound a whole heap different from his own childhood and youth. Betty bemoaned the fact that she seldom got to go into town, but he had been with the Jacksons almost a year before they took him to visit the nearest town. It was just how things were in that corner of the territory, there were few towns and mainly just scattered farms and homesteads.

'Do you ever think of your real parents?' said Betty.

'You mean my Cheyenne parents? Yes, I remember them, particularly my mother. I was about eight, I suppose, when they were killed.'

'Who killed them?'

'Soldiers. It was near the end of the war.'

'What sort of soldiers?'

'Bluecoats, cavalry. They came to our village and killed everybody.'

'What, women and children too?'

'It was almost all women and children. They killed everyone. There were some survivors, but the next day, the soldier in charge had them killed as well, so that there would be no witnesses remaining. I was the only one out of the whole village who was not killed.'

'Jeez. I thought I had it hard and my parents just died of the cholera. Did you see your ma die?'

'I did. A soldier cut her down with

his sabre. He nearly took off her head.'

Betty looked sick. She said, 'I am sorry. I did not know.'

'There is no reason why you should.'

'Are you really going to sit here all night watching that man?' asked Betty.

'I don't see that I have another choice. If I close my eyes, he is apt to try and escape, probably killing us while doing so.'

'In that case, I think I shall sleep now. You will be all right just sitting here like this?'

Han smiled at her, the first time that he had done so properly since they had met. The effect was extraordinary; it lit up his whole face and made him look to the girl like a different person. He said, 'I am an Indian. It is what we Indians do best of all, just sitting like statues and not moving.'

Betty did something which surprised the both of them. She leaned over without warning and kissed him on the cheek. Then she scuttled away, her cheeks burning with embarrassment, but concealed by the darkness.

Sitting there, cradling the rifle in his arms, Han thought about Betty. She was irritating, it was true, but once you got to know her better, she was not bad company. The fire was dying down now, but it was not that cold and Han didn't feel inclined to take his eyes off Holt and go wandering round looking for more wood. Jed Holt was lying down, but Han could see his eyes glinting, so he was not yet asleep. Lying there with those sharp, mean little eyes, he put Han in mind of a rattlesnake.

It was a long night. Han's eyes did not close once. Every time he looked closely at Holt, he could just about make out that his eyes were not closed either. It was a fair bet that the man was lying there hoping for a chance to get free. Having Betty sleeping a few yards away helped Han to remain awake, too. It was not just for his own sake, but also for the girl's that he had to watch over the killer. If he once gained the upper hand or got ahold of a gun, there could be little doubt that Holt would kill Betty as well as Han.

The three of them had a meagre breakfast, consisting mainly of the scraps and remains of the previous night's meal. Han rekindled the fire and they brewed coffee after they had eaten. Both Jed Holt and Han looked tired and were in bad moods. Betty, who was the only one of them who had got any sleep that night, was perky and gay. 'Do you think we'll reach Hopetown today?' she asked brightly, while they were drinking their coffee.

'I think so,' said Han. 'By my reckoning, we should be only twenty miles or so from it. What do you think?' He turned to Holt. The older man just shrugged and did not reply. Han could not really blame him. Holt's prospects were not very good once he had reached town. Pete McGuire had said that it was certain-sure that warrants were out naming both the Holt brothers in connection with crimes that were hanging matters.

Han and Betty tidied up the area where they had been camping and then they all mounted up. Han had observed that Holt did not seem to have any real and natural emotions, but just switched different manners on as he saw that they would serve him. When he had suspected that he could win the girl round to his side against Han, he had been courtly and charming, but now that he knew that there was nothing to be gained by this, he had dropped it completely. He ignored Betty entirely this morning. It was the same with the way that he was with Han. He had been agreeable yesterday when he could see a percentage in it, but now he made no effort at all to be in the least bit pleasant.

The sky had clouded over and there was a hint of a chill in the air. Han was thinking that he would not be at all sorry to get indoors when they reached Hopetown. He had enough left for a couple of nights in a boarding-house and then he was going back to his parents' house. He supposed that he would have to run the farm alone, now that they were dead.

Without any warning, Holt reined in his horse and said, 'This is as far as I go.'

'What are you talking about?' asked Han.

'Just what I say. I am going no further.' Holt then proceeded to get off his horse and sit on the ground. Now if he had bolted, then Han might, just might, have been able to fire at him. He plain could not shoot a man who was just sitting there on the ground, grinning up at him.

'Holt, you stop this foolishness. You know we are going on to Hopetown today.'

'You go right ahead. I ain't coming.'

Han sat there for a few seconds, trying to come up with the best plan. He decided that a good start would be to get down off his own horse with his rifle. He had no clear idea of what he might do after that, but at least it was a beginning. Holt was sitting there on his left, about twenty feet from him. As Han dismounted, he had his back to the man for a second and that was time enough for Jed Holt to spring to his feet, run over to Betty and grab ahold of her leg. She screamed in surprise and by the time that Han was off his horse and had his rifle in his hands ready to fire, Holt had managed to drag the girl off her pony. He whirled her round and tried to get his hands round her throat, crying, 'You come nigh to us, boy, and I am going to choke the life out of this little bitch!'

That leastways was his plan, although he had not taken into account that Betty, like Han, had grown up on a farm and was pretty lithe and muscular in her own way. Perhaps Holt had been misled by her simpering and giggling, but, as his hands scrabbled for her neck, the girl jabbed him in the belly, hard, with her elbow. He cursed and lunged forward, trying to use his weight against her. She half turned and raked her fingernails down the side of his face. As she did so, Han came up to the pair of them, reversed his rifle and slammed the butt into the side of Jed Holt's head. It is only in books that such an action will end with the person served so, promptly keeling over in a faint. The pain only enraged Holt all the more and he made another grab at Betty. Han had to crack him on the skull another couple of times before he lay still; whether dead or merely unconscious, Han neither knew nor cared.

10

Han helped the girl to her feet and they moved away from Holt. Cocking his rifle, Han kept it aimed right at the outlaw. He might look harmless enough lying there, but there was no limit to the tricks he might be up to in his frenzied efforts to avoid answering for his crimes.

'Are you all right?' Han asked the girl.

'I will answer,' she replied, 'although I would not like to go through another such wrestling match in a hurry.'

'It looked to me as though you was getting the better of that contest. Where did you learn to fight so?'

'I had to take care of myself. I had several people try it on with me, as you might say. A girl had to learn to protect her honour.' She giggled.

'Well you surely managed to hold

your own with that son of a . . . gun. Tell me, would you object overmuch if I was to shoot him now, before he recovers like?'

'You are joking?'

'I am joking a bit. I would still like to shoot him though.'

At length, Holt showed signs of recovering his senses. This was indicated by groans, profanities and a prolonged bout of swearing about Betty and Han. When he showed no signs of easing up on the tirade, which contained some of the coarsest language which Han had ever in his life heard, he said sternly to Holt, 'Recollect yourself, there is a lady present.'

'Lady, you say? Where is she? I don't see none such.'

'We are going to be moving off directly,' said Han, 'so you had best collect yourself and accept your fate like a man.'

'Yes,' said Holt bitterly, 'it is all well and good your talking of us both being men, but I will take oath that you would not durst face me, just the two of us together, if my hands were free.'

Han laughed. 'That is foolish talk, Holt. Your hands were free that night I grabbed ahold of your shirt and threatened to blow your head off. Or had you forgot that?'

'No, I had not forgotten that. There will be a reckoning for it as well.'

'Not in this world. Come, get back on your horse.'

'Suppose I refuse?'

'Then before God, I will come over there and kick your ass, begging your pardon, Betty.'

'Don't mind me,' said Betty. 'It is a word which I have heard before.'

Han stood up. 'Come, Holt, what will you have?' A thought struck him. 'Don't think that you will be able to goad me into shooting you, so you can escape the hangman's noose. I will do no such thing. Either you get on that horse peaceable, or I will knock you out again and then truss you up like a hog and carry you on the horse in that wise. Is that really how you would wish to enter Hopetown?'

After a little further grumbling and not a few curse-words, Holt mounted his horse and the three of them set off again. Now a circumstance which none of them marked was that somewhere along the line, the tin star had fallen from Han's shirt and lay back there at the scene of the tussle.

The fight had improved Jed Holt's spirits, as did anything in the line of violence. His mood might have improved, but this was more than could be said for his general appearance, which now presented a shocking spectacle. In view of what happened that day, Han later wondered if this whole episode had been designed with that end in mind. At any rate, in addition to the scratches across his cheek, Holt was pretty bruised on one side of his face where Han had swung the rifle butt at him. Blood was also trickling down his face from a cut which had been inflicted in the same way on his scalp.

Add to this the dirt and twigs which were all over his hair and upper body and the man presented a dreadful aspect to the world. Han noticed it when Holt turned to address remarks to him from time to time.

'Land sakes, Holt, your face is a sight to behold. Why did you make all that necessary?'

Jed laughed at that. 'If you cannot bear to see what you have done, then my advice to you would be not to do it. You struck me with your gun and this is the consequence.'

'You were purely sitting up and begging for it, as you well know. If we come to a stream or something, I am amenable to your washing away some of the blood and freshening yourself up somewhat. If we enter town with you in that state, it will make people think that I have been knocking you around.'

Holt turned round and bestowed an ill-favoured smile upon the young man. 'Why, that is precisely right. Folks might very well think such a thing.'

'Meaning that you will be able to appear in the role of victim? Yes, I see that this would do you no harm.'

'Tell me, boy,' said Holt, 'I heard you last night talking to that girl about your folks. I was right then that they died at Sand Creek? Is that why you came hunting for me and my brother? On account of losing not one set of parents, but two?'

Reluctantly, Han answered, 'Yes, if you will know the truth.'

'What would have befallen you if I had not ridden by that day? You would have just carried on tilling those fields? You know, I suppose, that we did you a favour there?'

'Shut up, Holt. I do not wish to hear anything which you have to say touching upon the subject.'

Holt continued as though Han had not spoken. 'The way I see it, those old folks were just about tuckered out. They could not have worked for much longer and yet might have needed taking care of for years before they died. That burden would have fallen upon you. You would have been working the land for all the hours God sent and then nursing a pair of useless old folk into the bargain. No chance to go out courting a girl, marrying and suchlike.'

'I have told you to leave this alone, Holt,' said Han in a queer, tight voice.

'See though, what the situation is now that you find yourself in? You have a farm, a house, no dependants to fret about, no relatives liable to come begging for your aid. Seems to me that your prospects is much improved since me and my brother relieved you of those useless mouths.'

The shot echoed across the bleak landscape. The ball from Han's rifle passed only inches from Holt's head, so close that he heard it pass by, buzzing like a bee. Han rode up and faced the man.

'I am not to be pushed into killing you, Holt, but that is not to say that I will not put a bullet in you, somewhere like your ankle or knee. I tell you now, before God, that if you say one more single word about my parents, I will do so. You will hang none the less for having a broken ankle and I am telling you that I am the very boy to give it you. What do you say? Will you carry on down this road and see what it brings you?'

'I reckon not,' said Holt and they continued travelling.

After they had gone another mile or two down the road, Holt said, 'Still and all, it is a thing to consider. People treat those like my brother and me as mad killers, but there is another side to the case.'

Unable to resist his curiosity, Han enquired, 'How do you figure that?'

'We weed out those who are often no use to society or their own selves. The weak, the old, the foolish. You could say that Eli and me have been like farmers, taking out the weeds and cutting back weak plants. I think that we deserve some recognition for this.'

'I would say this,' said Han slowly, 'it

seems to me that maybe they will not hang you after all. Perhaps they will instead shut you up in a mad asylum. You and that brother of yours were mad dogs. You are trying to make your crimes sound more than they were. They were dirty acts by two dirty and worthless men. You asked a couple of nights ago if I had ever been to a hanging. I will tell you now that I aim to come to see you hanged, Holt. I want to make sure that they make a good job of the business. You will end up like your brother, in an unmarked grave.'

He dropped back a little to ride by Betty's side for a spell. She said to him, 'You should not set mind to what he says. He is crazy as a coot.'

'Yes, this is so, but the worst of it is that there could be some slight grain of truth in what he says. Have you noticed how people like to read books about outlaws and robbers? They do not show any such enthusiasm for books about dirt farmers and storekeepers. Perhaps he does have some sort of noble calling.

It would explain much.'

'Don't listen to him. What happens when we get to Hopetown and hand him over to the sheriff? Do you really want to part from me for good? We can if you will. I should not have buffaloed you into bringing me along on this trip. It was not nice of me.'

'Let us get rid of this man first and then we can perhaps talk about it. I cannot think straight today. You will recall that I did not get a wink of sleep last night for having to watch yon villain.'

For the next three hours, they carried on along the track leading to Hopetown. All three of them were tired and none was in the best of moods. Despite her making light of the fight with Holt, Betty had been badly shaken by the experience and was still frightened when she thought of how the affair could have ended. She was also thinking on the future and trying to make out how Han was inclined to her and, just as importantly, how she was inclined towards him. Han was brooding that he had let Holt provoke him into opening fire. More than that, he was turning over the man's words in his mind, those to the effect that Han was better off now than he would have been if he faced the future prospect of caring for Esther and Patrick. There was undeniable truth in it and he did not wish to face the fact.

As for Jed Holt, it is not really possible to say what was going through his mind as their journey drew nigh to its final destination. He was like a cornered animal, seeking only a way out of the trap into which he had fallen. Since he had no weapons at his disposal and was covered by a young man armed with two guns who had cause to hate him, the only thing open to him was to probe at the boy's defences with his words. Whether this would be sufficient to find a weak spot before they reached Hopetown was by no means certain. Still and all, Jed Holt had never been a quitter and he was not about to fall into that habit at this late stage of his life.

Han called a rest at midday and they finished off the half-loaf of bread which remained. There was just about enough coffee for a single cup each, although no sugar to go in it. Betty kindled a small fire and did the necessary. Once again, Han made sure that Holt sat at a distance from him and the girl and he ate and drank with the rifle in his lap, never taking his eyes off Holt, even when he was chatting to Betty.

'Boy, there is a thing that I would know,' said Holt, after they had drunk their coffee, 'and that is this. You are an Indian and you are helping out the white man's law and his whole system. Does that not sit ill with your conscience? Wasn't it the white man who killed your family all those years ago?'

'It was white *men* not the white man. There is good and bad in all types. Are you not proof of that? There are bad Indians as well. This girl here had her kin killed by such and her home burned down.'

'How's that? I have not heard this story.'

Betty related the story of her capture by the Kiowa and Han's part in freeing her. After he had listened intently, Holt said, 'You are something else again, you know that, boy? I do not think that you and me are all that different. That is just exactly the way that I too would have handled that show.'

'Except,' observed Han, 'you would have killed the men and stolen both ponies instead of just the one. I managed the whole business without shedding blood.'

Holt laughed and was about to say something more, when Han cut in, saying, 'I am up to all your games, Holt. You hope to delay matters by talking endlessly like a woman, while you hope that something might turn up to prevent you being delivered to the sheriff in Hopetown. It will not answer. Within a few hours, we will be there and I will be rid of you.'

Holt offered no further resistance to mounting his horse and riding on in the direction of the town. For most of the travelling, they had seen no other rider, but now they began to see one or two men passing by; not actually on the same track as them, but maybe half a mile on either side. Han took this to be a sign that they were getting closer to the town. Halfway through the afternoon, they saw three men riding towards them. As they came closer, they looked to be ordinary, respectable folk about their business. It was now that Holt made his last desperate throw for freedom.

Betty and Han were talking about this and that, although the Indian did not take his eyes off the man ahead of him. With no warning whatsoever, Holt spurred his horse on towards the approaching men, crying, 'I am a federal officer! This Indian has killed my men and taken me captive. I call upon you by the power authorized to me by law to assist me in apprehending an offender. You have a legal duty to aid me.'

This was such an unexpected turn of events, that Han was at a loss to know how to proceed. So he just carried on riding forward, not at all sure what would be the outcome of Jed Holt's latest gambit. He pulled up sharply when one of the men drew his pistol and said, 'That's far enough now.'

'You fool,' said Han, 'I am a deputy and this man is under arrest and being escorted to the sheriff's office in Hopetown. The boot is all on the other foot and it is me you should be assisting. That man is a dangerous killer.'

This new claim seemed to throw the men into some confusion, which was not at all lessened when Holt said confidently, 'Him a deputy? Where is his badge, if that is so? And, more to the point, did you ever hear of an Indian being given the authority to arrest a white man?'

212

Han glanced down and was dismayed to see that his star had fallen off at some time in the past. The other three men were looking at him with no friendly eye and Holt, observing this, decided to follow up his advantage. 'Look well upon him,' he said. 'He is a Cheyenne dog soldier and he and his fellows ambushed my patrol. All were killed but me. I was off duty, which is how I am not in uniform, but I am a cavalry officer. I was tracking down a party of Cheyenne who have been a-murdering and looting all over this territory. If you do not assist us in this enterprise, it could be your wives or daughters next who are seized and sold into slavery.'

It was obvious that Holt had not dreamed up this pack of lies on the spur of the moment. He had been putting together the story all day and just waiting for the chance to tell it.

'I have in my pocket here a letter from the sheriff of Tribulation, which gives me authority and names this man as Jed Holt, a notorious wrongdoer.'

'Jed Holt?' said one of the men. 'Are you saying that this here is Jed Holt?'

These were the very last words that the man spoke in the course of his life. Seeing that this particular gamble was about played out and that his hand was not worth betting on, Holt rode up to the man who had just spoken, reached with both hands for the pistol that he wore, pulled it from the man's holster and shot him dead. Then he turned to face Han.

The shot had spooked the horses and they all began to jitter around and whinny. Holt's own horse reared and bucked, but he managed to stay on. He could not get a bead on Han because of it, giving that young man an opportunity to reach out his rifle and draw down on Holt. As he did so, one of the other men, seeing his partner gunned down, drew his own pistol and fired at Holt, who shot back. Neither of them were hit.

While this was going on, Han drew

down on Holt and called upon him to throw down his gun. Instead, Holt tried to steady his horse which was now rearing again. He looked as though he were hoping only to get off a shot at Han, who seeing this, fired once. The bullet took Holt in the shoulder, low down and towards his chest. Holt dropped his pistol and clutched at the wound. Then his horse jittered again and he fell heavily to the ground, where he lay winded.

Han, who was mightily angry at how the intervention of the three men had precipitated the bloodletting, rode up and pulled out Pete McGuire's letter. The two surviving men read it, grim looks on their faces as they saw the real state of play.

'Well,' said one to the other, 'it looks like a true bill. What do you say?' The other nodded. Then the man who had spoken turned apologetically to Han. 'I am sorry about this, but you will allow that it looked mighty strange to see a Cheyenne holding a white man at gunpoint in this way. I am sorry that we read it wrong.'

Down on the ground, where he was lying, Holt called out, 'I am done for, you bastards. You let that Indian kill me.'

'I reckon we'll be moving on,' said one of the men who had nearly caused Han's death and allowed Holt to escape, 'not wishing to be mixed up with the law and such. It would not do for a man in my position.'

'After causing this death, you would just up and leave?' asked Han in amazement.

'I am not a one for sitting around in courts and attending inquests, and neither, I'll warrant, is my friend here. So, if there is nothing else?'

'What about your partner?' asked Han, pointing at the dead man.

'He is not right close to us, to speak honestly,' said the more talkative of the two. 'It is not like he is my brother or something of that sort. Besides which, he is dead and there is little I can do to remedy the situation.'

'What do you say I should do with his body?' asked Han.

'Well, you are apparently a deputy and I guess that it is part of your duties to make provision for such contingencies. You may take him with you to Hopetown or leave him here. It is nothing to him any more; he is dead.'

'Why, you cold-blooded piece of . . . ' began Han, but then stopped. 'All right then, ride on. I hope that you are both satisfied with this day's work, which has cost two men their lives.'

Holt protested from where he lay, 'I ain't dead yet!' Then he gave a sharp groan of pain and doubled up in agony.

After the two men had left, Han got down from his pony and looked at Holt's wound. Even now, he did not trust the man, half expecting that he would make another attempt to seize a gun and escape. A quick glance told him that the bullet had not hit the shoulder at all, but was a deal lower. It had not just passed through, but was clearly lodged deep inside Holt's chest. He shook his head. 'I don't see that there is much that I can do for you. I am guessing that the bullet has entered your lung or is near your heart. I am sorry.'

'What's to do then?' Holt asked. He had a spasm of coughing and Han saw flecks of blood spray from his mouth. He had no training in such matters, but it looked to him as though that surely meant that the wounded man's lung was shot through.

'We will not ride on,' said Han gently. 'I will try to make you comfortable here. I am sorry it turned out like this.'

'Well I ain't,' said Holt. 'There are worse deaths a man could suffer. From all that I am able to collect, this will not take long.'

Han turned to Betty, who was looking sick and shaken. 'Bring me the blanket from my saddle-roll. And the canteen.' Turning to Holt, he said, 'Is there anything I can do for you?'

'I am cold. That blanket would not come amiss.'

Han set aside his pistol, it being too late to fret about such. He then tucked the blanket around Holt, just like he was tucking him up in bed. The man looked up at him. His face was ashen and he was trembling. After coughing up a little more blood, Holt said, 'I am not sorry that it was you who shot me. When I stood there that night, with your gun pushed against my neck, I knew then that you would be the death of me.'

'Don't talk,' said Han, 'you are using up your strength. Would you have me read a psalm to you or say a prayer? I know a heap of such from my parents.'

Holt tried to smile, but it turned into a grimace of pain. 'No, I can't say that I would be comforted none by such a thing at this time. I would like a sip from that canteen though if you could lift me up a mite.'

Han supported the dying man round the shoulders and helped him take a sip of water. This provoked a paroxysm of spluttering, which sent blood all down the man's shirtfront. 'I am failing,' he said. 'I am sorry for killing your folks, but I don't suppose that signifies now.'

'It does,' said Han softly. 'It surely does. Can I get you anything else?'

There was no reply. Holt had laspsed into unconsciousness and he lay there for another five minutes in Han's arms before breathing his last. Betty stood still while this was happening, pale with shock.

11

After Holt had died, Han lowered his body to the ground and stood up. 'This is the hell of a business. I would not have looked to kill him like that. I did not mean to do so, but I can't see that I had another choice.'

Betty said, 'If you had not done it, I think that he would cheerfully have shot us all, if that was what it took to get him free from here.'

'Yes, I made the same calculation, which is why I shot him. I am still sorry that I did it though.'

Some of her pertness returning, Betty said, 'You would have been a sight sorrier had he shot us, I reckon.'

'That at least is true,' said Han.

There remained the vexing problem of how to proceed from this point onwards. One way would have been just to abandon Jed Holt and the unknown dead man and ride off. There were two things against this course of action. In the first place, Han had had quite a connection with this man. Not a good one maybe, but nevertheless their paths had crossed and then run side by side. He could not just leave him here like a dead animal. Then again, he had engaged to take the man to Hopetown and hand him over to the sheriff. If he left him here and went off, it would look for sure as though he had killed the man out of hand and bolted. Han did not want such a thing said of him, even by strangers.

In the end, he and Betty succeeded in loading both Holt and the dead stranger on the back of Holt's horse, the other two men having taken away the stranger's horse in the confusion following the shooting. Han tied their ankles to their wrists to keep them from falling off. It looked ugly, for all that it was the most practical way of accomplishing his purpose. He did not like to see men treated like animals in this way, but there was no other way of doing it.

★ ★ ★

As they rode along, Han reflected upon the strange way that the oath which he had made to the Great Spirit had, almost against his wishes, been fulfilled. After failing to kill Holt in the saloon that night, Han had forsworn his vengeance and resolved to allow the law to deal with the man. He had felt a twinge of uneasiness as the time, at the thought that he might be breaking his oath. But in the end, he had indeed killed the last of the men who were responsible for his parents' deaths, just as he had sworn to do.

Han turned over in his mind what Jed Holt had said just before he died. He had said that he knew Han would be the death of him. Had he really had some inkling of his fate, a realization of what would come to pass? These melancholy thoughts were interrupted by Betty, who had a more practical concern.

'Do you think that you will get into trouble for this?' said Betty. 'When we reach town, I mean? You don't think that anybody will say that you shot Holt without cause.'

This had not occurred to Han. He thought the question over in his mind. At last, he said, 'I do not look for that to happen. If, as the sheriff in Tribulation says is likely, there is news that Holt is wanted, then I think that folk will understand what came to pass. Besides, I have a witness.'

It was slow going. There was no question of proceeding at more than a walk with the two men on the one horse. A couple of times they had to stop, because one or the other of the corpses swung round so that the body was hanging round the belly of the horse, with the ankles and wrists on the top side, resting on the saddle. Not only did this look gruesome, it slowed down the horse. It was evening before they got to Hopetown.

It was a fair-sized place with a railroad station, telegraph and all that a modern town could require. The sight of an Indian, accompanied by a white girl and two corpses was a novel one and folks stopped dead in the streets to stare at the odd sight. More than that, they called people from their houses to come and see. A crowd of shouting boys surrounded them at one point, making what Han supposed were intended to be Indian war whoops. He had to enquire several times before he was able to discover where the sheriff's office was. This was because the first person he asked, a woman, hurried off in panic.

At length, they found the office, which by a great mercy was not closed for the day. Han and Betty dismounted, tethering the horse with the dead men on it outside. They went in and Han handed the sheriff the letter from Pete McGuire. He read it in a leisurely fashion, like a man who has all the time in the world.

After mastering the contents of the letter to his own satisfaction, he put it down on the desk and looked up at the two young people. 'So you have been sent by Pete McGuire, hey? Well, I make no bones about telling you that he is a lazy son of a bitch and a dishonest fellow to boot. How come he did not bring this dangerous robber here himself?'

Han shrugged. 'I could not say, sir. He asked me to do so and I have brought him.'

'Well, where is he?'

'He is outside.'

'What the devil have you left him out there for? If this really is Jed Holt, he will be halfway to Kansas by now.'

'I don't think so, sir. You see there was a mishap along the way and he is now dead.'

'First I want to see the body. I know the Holts by sight. This would not be the first time that somebody tried to sell me a cat in a sack and claim reward money of some body belonging to the Lord knows who. Show me.'

'Reward money?' said Han. 'You mean that we might get a reward for bringing him in?'

'Let's take it one step at a time. Like I say, first off is where I want to be sure that this really is one of the famous Holt brothers.'

They went out to where the horses were tethered. A large crowd was gathered round the bodies. The sheriff said, 'Come on, you fellows, move away now. What do you think this is, a carnival sideshow or something of that sort? Move clear, I tell you.' He unceremoniously lifted up the heads of the two dead men by grasping their hair. He took a good long look at Holt.

'All right, let's go back in the office and make medicine. You loafers move away from the front of my office now, you hear?'

Once they were all three back in the sheriff's office, he asked them to explain how Holt had died and who the other dead person might be. Betty and Han took it in turns to explain how it had been. When they had finished, he said, 'Well, that sounds like the truth to me. At any rate, one of those two men is Jed Holt, of that there is no doubt. Now, this is where the knife meets the bone, as they say. There are two rewards for Holt. One is an official one, for the amount of five hundred dollars. Seeing that you would not have known of this unless I told you, I think it fair if we split that down the middle, me taking half and the same to you. How does that sound?'

Han said slowly, 'I think that that is very fair, sir. I did not look to profit from this business, seeing it as my duty, so to speak.'

'Well ain't you the virtuous one?' said the sheriff. 'There is more though and I will put you on to this, although it profits me nothing. Holt killed some fellow up in Denver City and the family offered a five hundred dollar reward on their own account for his capture, alive or dead. I will give you the details and also a chit from me to say that you brought him in dead. That should be all you need to secure the money.'

'That is right good of you, sir,' said Han. 'You mean that you will get nothing from it?'

'I am not a greedy man, son,' said the sheriff. 'I have just made myself two hundred and fifty for sitting here and doing precious little, while you brought Jed Holt here and nearly got yourself killed in the process. I would say that you have earned that money. Come back tomorrow morning and I will pay out the money.'

Han and Betty could hardly believe what had happened. They went out into the street and, ignoring the curious stares of those still hanging round outside the sheriff's office, walked down the street a way. Betty said, 'Tell me straight, Han, do you want us to part company for good and all here? I will be able to find something here, work or what have you, if that is to be the way of it.'

Han looked at her and she fancied that now that this other business had been dealt with, he was looking at her differently. 'If you want to come with me for a while, maybe stay at my place when I go back, then you are welcome to do so.' It struck him that he sounded ungracious and he added, 'You are more than welcome. I would like it very much.'

We do hope that you have enjoyed reading this large print book.

Did you know that all of our titles are available for purchase?

We publish a wide range of high quality large print books including:
Romances, Mysteries, Classics
General Fiction
Non Fiction and Westerns

Special interest titles available in large print are:
The Little Oxford Dictionary
Music Book, Song Book
Hymn Book, Service Book

Also available from us courtesy of Oxford University Press:
Young Readers' Dictionary
(large print edition)
Young Readers' Thesaurus
(large print edition)

For further information or a free brochure, please contact us at:
Ulverscroft Large Print Books Ltd.,
The Green, Bradgate Road, Anstey,
Leicester, LE7 7FU, England.
Tel: (00 44) **0116 236 4325**
Fax: (00 44) **0116 234 0205**

THE DEVIL'S ANVIL

Steve Hayes

Two kill-crazy McClory cousins have busted out of Yuma Pen, heading for Indian Territory. Somebody has to bring them in — and the job falls to Deputy US Marshal Liberty Mercer, who sets off to run the outlaws to ground. But to reach the McClory stronghold in Silver Rock Canyon, Mercer and her makeshift posse — Raven Bjorkman, her old friend; Latham Rawlins, brother of Liberty's one-time love Latigo; and the crooked Dunn brothers — must cross the deadly, searing desert known as the Devil's Anvil . . .

COUGAR TRACKS

Owen G. Irons

Former US Army scout Carroll Cougar desires only to live peacefully on his Twin Creek ranch. Then a letter from the President arrives. Enemy forces plan to assassinate General Crook, and the Army wants Cougar back to take out the threat . . . The old scout has no desire to return to military life. But when he learns that Crook's would-be killer is none other than Solon Reineke, he swiftly saddles up to answer the call of duty. For Reineke is the man who murdered Carlina Polk, a woman Cougar loved . . .